William Taylor

Our South American Cousins

South American Cousins

BY

WILLIAM TAYLOR,

Author of "Seven Years Street Preaching in San Francisco,"
"Christian Adventures in South Africa," "Four
Years Campaign in India," Etc., Etc.

NEW YORK:

NELSON AND PHILLIPS.

LONDON:

HODDER AND STOUGHTON.

1879.

INTRODUCTION.

THE two Grand Divisions of the New World, discovered contemporaneously, their histories parallel in time, peopled by races derived from a common stock, having a family surname in common, and linked by a band of Nature's own making, may be regarded as Sister Continents.

Their respective populations are kindred—cousins each to the other, in the great Race Family that is spread abroad over the globe.

I have just returned from a friendly visit among these South American Cousins of ours, and have recorded in the following pages what I have learned about them, and about their great country. The drapery of my illustrative facts, incidents, and pictures of real life will be purely English, and not Spanish; so you may read audibly for the entertainment of your friends without fear of stumbling on foreign words.

CONTENTS.

6 CONTENTS.

Our South American Cousins.

I.

My Voyage to South America.

On the 16th of October, 1877, I bought for myself and for Bro. T——, a fellow-minister, a through ticket from New York to Callao, Peru, and embarked on the Pacific Mail Steamship Company's steamer, the *Acapulco*, bound for Aspinwall.

I did not wish our friends to come to see us off, and they didn't come. I always prefer to come in and go out as quietly as possible; indeed, coming and going all the time, as I have been doing more than a quarter of a century, my friends could not anticipate my changes.

On the eve of one of my departures from London to Australia, a gentleman said: "Mr. Taylor, what is your address now?"

"I am sojourning on the globe, at present, but don't know how soon I shall be leaving."

I remember many occasions, however, in lands remote, where my friends did as St. Paul's friends were wont to do—accompany me to the ship, "and sorrowed most of all that they should see my face no more."

About fifteen years ago, after a successful soul-saving campaign in Tasmania, I preached in Launceston, on the eve of my departure, to a crowded house, at 6 A.M. The whole congregation, including some hundreds of persons who had recently received the Saviour, accompanied me to the ship. They stood on the shore, and sang hymns, and waved adieus till I passed from view.

Once, on leaving Sydney, Australia, some of my friends chartered a steamer, and out through that most commodious and beautiful harbor in the world, escorted the ship on which I was passenger, singing hymns and cheering vociferously. The leader of that loving company was a Crown Prosecutor, and a nephew of the Duke of Wellington. I fully appreciated the kindness of my friends, but hid away from the gaze of men as soon as I could.

Well, there was nothing of that sort when

Bro. T—— and I bade adieu to our native land, last October.

Indeed, for reasons satisfactory to ourselves, we embarked as steerage passengers. Patrick said to the Judge, "I have thirteen reasons to assign for my father's non-appearance in court. The first reason is that he has been dead for three weeks." "The second reason is "—" That one is sufficient," interrupted the Judge. So, for our appearance in the steerage, one reason may suffice. By helping to send missionaries to my work in India, for the last two years, together with heavy traveling and family expenses, my funds were so far spent that I was obliged to go third-class to see my cousins, or not go at all; paying, as I do, my traveling expenses out of my own pocket, and not out of the pockets of my friends. A first-class ticket from New York to Callao costs two hundred and seventy-five dollars in gold, a third-class ticket, one hundred dollars. I believed, too, that my dignity would keep for eighteen days in the steerage. I have made over sixty sea-voyages first-class, at the cost of enough of my hard-earned dollars to give my sons a university education and keep me comfortably the rest of my life. I thus quietly maintained the appearance, as well as the real dignity of a gentleman, and never begrudged a dollar of it, except in a few voyages with the "Peninsula and Oriental S. S. Company," when they included enormous bills for "wine and spirits" in the cost of passage-tickets. On one voyage, my ticket from Suez, in Egypt, to Melbourne, Australia, cost me six hundred dollars. Later, I paid six hundred dollars for a ticket from London to Sydney.

I said to the agent, "You charge me more than one hundred dollars extra on a single voyage for 'drinks,' when I don't drink a drop, either of wine or spirits."

He replied, "All pay alike; wine and spirits are furnished for all the passengers, and they can drink, or not, as they like." I didn't "like it, but I had to lump it," and pay the bill.

Men of fortune, and business men who are making money, ought, by sea and land, to travel first-class, not only for the sake of their own respectability, but to support the carrying companies who provide such grand facilities for the traveling public and for the commerce of the world.

But the men and women who cannot afford, from their own funds, to travel first-class, should be humble enough, without any feeling of disgrace, for it is not disgraceful, to travel third-class, unless they prefer to play "would, if I could," and go second.

I can't say that I took naturally to the steerage. I mingled with the crowd "aft," till the ship "got under way," and then quietly advanced to the forward part of the vessel, where we get the first snuff of the pure breezes, and escape all the accumulated odors of the ship which make the first-class ladies and gentlemen so sick.

Now, as the bell rings for our departure, let us review the situation. See that Irish girl hanging round the neck of her lover, weeping vociferously. He tears himself away, and hurries off the ship. She rushes through the crowd in pursuit of him, screaming aloud in broken sobs and cries. An officer of the ship arrests her on the gangway and fetches her back. Poor young woman! she seems quite inconsolable.

Here are two blooming brides with their bridegrooms. One pair of them emigrating to California, the other are on a bridal tour to visit kindred in Virginia City, Nevada, by the "Robin-Hood-Barn" route.

See the beautiful woman in that group
She seems in appearance to be on the sunny
side of thirty; she is the mother of thirteen
children, and, with her kind husband, and
loving sons and daughters, all smiling and
happy, she is returning to California—a Portuguese family just from a visit to their "faderland."

What sort of a shattered, tattered family
group is that? An old Irishman and his
wife. The poor old bag of bones sitting beside them is all that remains of their elder
brother, who sold all his possessions to raise
money for the passage of the lot of them to
California, where they hope to pick up gold
in the streets. Poor old souls, I do pity
them in my heart. If the Blessed Virgin un-
dertakes to provide for that lot in California,
she will not have much time to spare for
her poor children away back on the Emerald
Isle.

Let us speak to this sick woman lying on
the deck. The pretty little girl by her side
is her daughter. They have set out to meet
husband and father in San Francisco. She
is an intelligent lady, and was for years a
New England "school-marm." She is unable

to walk, but her spirit will sustain her infirmity, and she will, by the will of God, recover her health, and join her husband. We have here a crowd of representatives of many nationalities, but all seem cheerful; and we find the forward deck an enjoyable place, free and easy as a pic-nic party.

There goes the gong. Ho for John Chinaman, "his rattle!" "Supper, supper, ladies and gentlemen," shouts the colored caterer for the company. We all march to the music, and gather round our "common board"—it is a long "board" about three feet wide; our board is suspended by ropes from the beams of the upper deck. 'Tis said that people can eat more standing erect than in a sitting posture, so we stand shoulder to shoulder along both sides of the board. Each eater finds before him a tin cup and an iron spoon. A great boiler of tea is passed round, all sweetened and ready for use, and the cups are filled. This, with a huge panful of excellent "ship bread," makes up the supper supply. "Our board" is then run up to the ceiling, and sleeping-bunks are extemporized in all the available space between decks. The ladies have a large forward cabin for their own exclusive use, and not the slightest intrusion allowed. Having some blankets of our own, Bro. T——and I prefer a spread on the upper deck, so we commit ourselves to the care of our gracious Father, and sleep sweetly in the light of the stars.

There, with rising swell, cadence, and clatter, goes John's rattle again.

"Breakfast gentlemen, breakfast." So with a rush we all gather again "round the board." Tin plates, knives and forks, and the familiar tin cup. A great boiler of good sweetened coffee is passed round, and our cups are filled; hard tack, butter, boiled potatoes, and tough "junk" make up a very digestible breakfast. In all my voyages my only real trouble at sea has been from indigestion.

Breakfast at 9 A.M.; dinner extending through an hour from 5 to 6 P.M., with half a dozen courses of not very digestible food. Such varieties don't suit me. A simpler fare is better, somewhere between this custom of courses, and that of an eccentric English gentleman who invited his minister to dine with him, and set before him half a dozen courses of rabbits, dressed up in 'so many different ways, somewhat after the "firstly," "secondly," and "thirdly" fashion in which the Gospel had been served to him. At the close the minister returned thanks thus:

" Rabbits hot, and rabbits cold,
   Rabbits young, and rabbits old,
   Rabbits tender, and rabbits tough,
   Thanks to Providence we've had rabbits enough."

Sabbath morning, bright and lovely. I'll get out a hundred copies of Bro. Hasting's admirable little papers, and distribute them to the ship's company "fore and aft." So I go through with a call familiar in the streets at home, but surprising at sea—" Morning papers ! morning papers ! Hastings' illustrated ! "

" How were the papers received ? "

" With a smile, and a ' thank you sir. ' " Some of the first-class passengers exclaimed in surprise: "Halloo, here comes a new passenger." " Where did he come from ? " " He seems to have just dropped down from heaven."

At 10 A.M. we have the dress parade of all the sailors and servants in their Sunday clothes, for inspection by the captain, and at 11 A.M. we repair to the saloon for "Divine Service."

An officer, after the style of a "hop, skip,

and a jump," gets over the lessons and prayers
of the Episcopal service, and a padrè, of
medium calibre, discharges his ecclesiastical
cannon ; and we respond to John's gong, and
do ample justice to the "duff," but the old
junk was rather too tough for my teeth.

Ninth day out, "land ho !" See, in the twi-
light of morning, the dense foliage of the Isthmus of Darien; the soft fleecy clouds drink
in and reflect golden rays from the Orient; the
dolphins sport around us; we are nearing our
first port of debarkation. Here we are in
" Colon "—the Spanish name for Columbus.
Poor old Christopher, how he has been stripped
of his laurels ! even this little town, on a remote
bog of the Carribbean Sea, is not allowed
longer to bear his name, but must be called
" Aspinwall."

The last French Empress sent to this town,
as a present, a grand bronze statue of Columbus, which extends a protecting arm around
the beautiful but timidly crouching statue of
an Indian princess. It should be put upon a
much larger and more substantial pedestal
than the one on which it now stands.

This town has grown considerably since I
saw it twenty-one years ago.

Our ship's company are bestirring them-selves for departure. "Rail train leaves for Panama at 3 P.M."

Our Portuguese family have been patient and cheerful all the way. Our old Irish woman has been sea-sick, and "reaching" hid-eously at all hours, and the two poor old men have never been known to smile since we em-barked, but their place at the "board" has never been vacant. They mean business. The Irish girl who would not be consoled on parting with her lover, has been flirting with the young men all the way. Our sick "school marm" is convalescent.

"Bro. T——, if you'll stay 'with the stuff,' I'll take a hundred copies of 'Hasting's Illustrated,' and make a pastoral tour in the town. Yonder is a colored cousin of ours, with his truck, waiting for an honest job; I'll begin with him."

"Good morning, sir."

"Good morning, Captain."

"Can you read English?"

"O yes, sah."

"Let me hear you read a little from this paper." He reads readily, and I give him the paper to keep.

" Where did you learn to read?"

" In Jamaica, sah."

" In what part of Jamaica did you live?"

" In Kingston, sah."

"To what church did you belong in Kingston?"

"Coke's Chapel, sah; de Wesleyan Church, sah."

"I have preached in Coke's Chapel many times."

" Oh, dear sah, we glad to see you here. If you are come to hunt for de place where you are needed de most, den you has found de field you are huntin'."

Now a crowd of hungry fellows gather round, saying, " Give me a paper," " Please, sir, give me a paper."

" Can you all read?"

" Oh, yes, sah; but we don't get many books nor papers to read here, sah. No minister to speak to us, nor to care for us. Won't you stop and be our minister?"

"No, I am sorry to say, I am obliged to proceed on my journey to Peru this afternoon."

" We are very sorry. Can't you send us a good minister, to look after us?"

" If I send you one, can you support him?"

"Yes; we'll divide with him what we get, and he no lack any good thing."

"Very well; I will keep you in mind, and perhaps the Lord may bring me to a man who will be willing to come to live and labor with you."

So I proceed from street to street.

"Well, did you get rid of all your papers?"

"Oh, yes, indeed, and could have disposed of a hundred more, if I had had them. Many called across the street and from the second-story windows of their dwellings, begging for papers; and many want to know when a preacher can be sent to Colon. The most of the people of this town are from the West India Islands, especially from Jamaica, that being the nearest. All whom I met profess to be religious, having been connected with the various mission churches of their native land. Very few of them, I apprehend, have much spiritual life left, but they remember the days of old, and deplore their utter lack of pastoral care."

I visited a poor old woman, who was very sick, and said to her, "Have you been long ill?"

"Yes, minister; I have been sick long time."

"Does the blessed Jesus abide with you, and give you light and comfort?"

"Yes, minister, I pray to God every day; but my friends all gone, and I feel very lonesome." I prayed for the forlorn soul, and gave her financial relief.

Train whistling for departure. "All aboard for Panama!" Passengers, loaded with bananas, get to their places, and now for an excursion of nearly fifty miles through a dense jungle of tropical verdure. As we sweep along the track, we see small fields cleared, some for the pasturage of cattle—we see herds of them feeding in them now—others, for the cultivation of vegetables and fruits, especially bananas, which supply our New York markets. We pass a number of villages swarming with our sable cousins, living in apparent poverty, but cleanly clad, except the little urchins who have never yet had a thread of clothing, and all smiling with contentment.

As our train rolls through these forests, I think of my homeward passage from California, twenty-one years ago. My own dear wife and children were with me then. This was the first railroad my boys had seen.

When we slowly moved from the station at Panama, my dear little Charlie exclaimed, "Pa, where are the horses?"

Coming to a curve, I showed him the engine, saying, "There's the horse, Charlie, see how he snorts."

He gazed in great astonishment, and shouted, "Where did they get him?"

My precious boy has long since gone to the country where horses are not needed.

Here we come into the railway station of Panama, sweeping past files of Colombia's soldiers, muskets in hand for our protection. We, indeed, need no such defense, but they are fulfilling a promise of their government made to the railroad company a quarter of a century ago, to prevent the possible recurrence of mob violence, by which a few passengers then were badly battered.

Here we are mid the noise and confusion of another embarkation. The tug is waiting to convey passengers and their luggage to the steamship *Bolivia*, in which we are to proceed fifteen hundred miles to Callao. The *Bolivia* is one of the ships of the Pacific Steam Navigation Company.

"The Pacific Mail Steamship Company?"

No; "The Pacific Steam Navigation Company."

What Company is that?

The most powerful organization of its kind in the world, except, possibly, the Peninsula and Oriental Company may be equal to it. The fleet of the Pacific Mail Steamship Company contains nineteen steamships, with an aggregate registry of 57,122 tons. They have many magnificent ships, two of which, the *City of Peking*, and the *City of Tokio*, have each a registry of 5,080 tons.

The fleet of the Pacific Steam Navigation Company consists of forty-seven steamships, with an aggregate registry of 114,285 tons. Ten of their ships exceed 2,000 tons each; seven exceed 3,000, and six exceed 4,000 tons each, the largest reaching a tonnage of 4,666. The ships of this Company do the principal transportation of this coast, from Panama to Patagonia. Their largest ships clear from Callao and from Liverpool. They take, every fortnight, freight and passengers from the principal ports on the west coast, pass through the Straits of Magellan, touch at Montevideo, Rio de Janeiro, Bahia, Pernambuco, Lisbon, and Bordeaux, and proceed thence to Liverpool.

A few years ago the Chile government launched a line of twelve powerful steamships, in competition for the immense trade of this coast. Both companies sunk a large amount of money in the race, and finally came to an agreement that the two lines should employ the same agents, and have the same rate of charges; the accounts and proceeds of each to be kept separate.

The ships of both of these lines are usually loaded to their utmost capacity.

But when did this great Pacific Steam Navigation Company spring up?

Well, as early as 1844, William Wheelright, an enterprising American residing in Valparaiso, laid the foundation of it. Having matured his plans, and arranged with all the Republics of the west coast for their execution, he went to New York to secure the requisite capital and co-operation, but our men of means gave him the cold shoulder. He turned away from his own country in disappointment and went to England, and there succeeded, by small shares, in raising the funds, and the "Pacific Steam Navigation Company" was organized as the result.

Well, here we are still in the railway station at Panama, trying to get our portmanteaus from the luggage car. Nobody in this latitude seems to be in any hurry to push business.

We can carry everything we've got in our own hands, but here are two strong fellows waiting for a job, so we'll give them a chance.

"Where did you come from?"

"From Jamaica, sah."

"How long have you been here?"

"About twenty years, sah."

"Have you made your fortune yet?"

"Make a livin', sah. Times very dull here now, sah. Fortune out ob de question, sah."

"What church did you attend in Jamaica?"

"De Wesleyan Church, sah."

"What religious services do you have here?"

"None at all, sah, except de Roman Catolic, and we don't take no stock in dat concern, sah. We had a minister here some years ago, but de white people want to read de prars, sah, and de colored people want to sing, sah, and de two parties couldn't agree, sah, so de preacher he done gone away, sah."

"Can you colored people raise sufficient funds among yourselves to support a minister if you had one?"

"Oh yes, sah, if we had a good minister who would be kind to us, he get support plenty.

We have in Panama, and in the neighborhood
round about the city, at least one thousand
Jamaicans, and none of dem don't follow de
Catolic religion."

"Can your people get a suitable place for
meetings if a minister should be sent?"

"Yes, sah, quick if de minister come."

They don't take to reading prayers readily.
At a railroad opening celebration in the West,
a preacher read an eloquent prayer which he
had composed for the occasion; at the close
Sambo exclaimed, "Dah, dat de fust time de
Lord was ever written to on de important subject of railroads."

Poor perishing sheep in the wilderness! can
no man be found who will come and care for
their souls?

But would not a minister take Panama
fever, and die there?

Possibly, but the risk of life for him would
not be greater than that of hundreds of Europeans and Americans who reside there, and
who appear to be as healthy as the people of
New York. The United States Consul of
Aspinwall, Vice-Consul, and their families, who
have been there over five years, have had
no serious illness. Dr. Long, our Consul at

Panama, has been there, I think he told me over thirty years, and he is a fine specimen of vigorous, healthy old age. I saw scores of resident Europeans and Americans there, merchants and others, whose appearance is as healthful as that of persons in any other country. Strong drink, and the lustful excesses to which it leads, should answer for three-fourths of the mortality which has given fame to Panama.

"Yes," replied Bro. T——, "when I crossed this Isthmus before the railroad was built, I and another teetotaler, acting upon the advice of good, pious friends in New York, provided ourselves each with a bottle of brandy. We carefully selected the brand specially recommended as an antidote to the malaria of the Isthmus. We uncorked, and commenced to take the medicine as soon as we landed in Colon, and before the boatmen had rowed us up the Chagres River, we emptied our bottles, and had to get a fresh supply. It made both of us sick, and it was a wonder that we did not die, as many of our fellow-passengers did, as I believe, from the effects of brandy and excess in eating fresh tropical fruits, to the use of which they had never been accustomed."

" All aboard for the *Bolivia.*" We reached
our ship far down in the Panama Bay, after
miles of tug-steaming.

The *Bolivia* is a staunch iron ship of 1,925
tons register. She has three decks, with lofty
space between. The hurricane deck is covered
with canvas awnings fore and aft.

We third-class folks find our bunks ready
for us on the forward part of the main deck,
where we can enjoy the full sweep of the
breezes, so refreshing in tropical heat.

The first-class ladies and gentlemen have
their saloon and cabins on " the upper deck."

The regular hour for dinner is past, so we go
to the cook and get a good broiled steak prepared to order. We like our sleeping accommo-
dations better here than in the *Acapulco.* All
the passengers of our class have left us, except
a German watchmaker from La Pass, Bolivia.
He knows enough of English to give us much
valuable information about the interior of this
great country.

Here, in our new quarters, we have no
" board " around which to " gather." Each
passenger is provided with a tin cup, soup-pan,
and spoon. At 6 A.M., Cousin Cholo appears
with a pot of hot coffee and a box of hard-tack,

both of superior quality. At 10 A.M., the same rotund, thick-set young Indian presents himself with a great pot of beef-soup, potatoes, and "tack;" and at 6 P.M., he reappears with tack and tea. This is the regular daily fare; but each passenger is allowed to make a special arrangement with the cook and the baker, to suit his own taste.

Bro. T—— and I could have gotten on well with the bill of fare named, but we paid the cook five dollars for a daily dinner for eight days; roast beef, and a variety of vegetables piled together in one course on a large deep plate.

Sabbath, the 27th, the eleventh day out from New York, as the sun is sinking below the horizon of the great waters of the west, we enter the mouth of the Guayas River. Here it is about twenty miles wide; eighty miles up-stream, opposite the City of Guayaquil, it is about a mile in width at high tide.

Among our passengers are Mr. Mero, Mr. Warburton, and an old Texian California miner, whom we call "Texas," and several other Californians who have "seen better days." Mr. Mero, a Canadian, resides in Concepcion, Chile. He is a railroad engineer, and has been to Cali-

fornia seeking a more congenial home for himself and his Chileno wife and children. Unable to find a hole in our Golden State in which
to dig, and having spent money enough in
prospecting to buy a western farm, he is going
back to seek success and contentment in his
old business in Chile.

Mr. Warburton is an Englishman, by trade a
founder, who has been employed in many of
the great foundries of the United States for
years, always getting good wages; but he is a
"rolling stone" that gathers no moss.

"Texas" is the comical yarn-spinner for the
company. As we ascend this beautiful river,
he walks the hurricane deck, sniffs the air, and
gets off squibs about the fever-breeding region
we are entering. "O, Jupiter," he exclaims,
"did you ever smell the like of that since the
day you were born! I tell you what it is,
friends, if you take a few more sniffs of that
sort, you may just as well close up your accounts and prepare to leave."

Light ahead—the City of Guayaquil. What
an extraordinary light; brighter and brighter!
It must be an illuminated house, but at this
distance it presents the appearance of a great
sheet of flame, reflecting what appears like a

stream of fire far along the surface of the placid waters. Nearer still, we see the illumination of one great building, much after the fashion of the Hindūs. Now we hear the music—a full band and drum.

Monday morning. "What sort of an entertainment was that last night in the city?"

"It was an anniversary celebration of St. Simon's day; a grand fandango—the dancers danced all night."

Yes; I heard them every time I awoke, till the dawn of the morning—a pious Sunday night's exercise in honor of St. Simon. What Simon was that? Simon Peter, Simon the Pharisee, Simon the Leper, Simon Magus, Simon the Tanner, or some modern saint of that name? Nobody seems to know or care so much about the dead saint, as for the living sinners who grace the occasion with their presence.

Now for the ship's music; the instruments are four "steam winches" working all at once. Here we see one turning out a lot of freight from New York—large quantities of lard, bacon, crushed sugar, etc., and there goes a veritable cabinet organ. But what strikes the stranger is the shipment of more than two hundred tons of fruits for the Callao markets—pineapples, limes, lemons, oranges, mangoes, plantains, and bananas by the cord. The after half of the main deck is piled to the joists, leaving but a narrow path on each side next to the officer's cabins. The upper deck is packed in the same way, leaving the first-class passengers barely space enough for ingress and egress.

Halloo! they are taking down our bunks—what does this mean?

"All the third-class passengers must gather up their luggage, and go to the after part of the hurricane deck." So all are busy collecting their luggage, and preparing for an exodus to a higher region.

"Why do they want to clear us off this deck—we are getting on well here?"

"They want space for two hundred bullocks, to be taken aboard at Payta." So we "vamoose the ranch" to make room for the steers.

Well, here we are in our new quarters, covered with canvas duck; good, better, best; high above the fruit barricade that shuts in our unfortunate first-class fellow-passengers, the best ventilation in the ship, and the whole length of the hurricane deck as a promenade; but we have an immense accession to our numbers. After twenty-four hours' steaming, our anchor drops in the roadstead of Payta.

What a bleak coast; not a shrub, not a blade of grass to be seen, not even a stalk of cactus, that takes root in a rock and lives on the wind.

Introduced to Mr. Foulks, an American gentleman, who has lived four years in the Piura Valley, twenty miles distant. The city of Piura is a hundred miles inland. Twenty miles of the distance traversed by a railroad. It is a beautiful city, celebrated for its mineral springs —a resort of health-seekers from all parts of Europe. Mr. Foulks has come to receive his wife and two little sons, who came with us from New York — a happy meeting. Mrs. Foulks is a member of the Dutch Reformed Church, and will, I hope, let her light shine in the dark vales of Piura. Mr. Foulks says the valleys of Piura are as fruitful as the garden of Eden, both in the variety and quality of their productions.

Here come the bullocks from Mr. Foulks' "garden of Eden."

The lighters for conveying freight to and from the ship are simply rafts of "balsa wood" logs, said to be buoyant as cork. I have just counted seventy huge beef cattle on a single raft, surrounded by a railing, a real "corral." The cattle are tied each by a rope to the railing. Now we shall see the process of slinging them from the raft to the deck of the ship. I suppose they will belt them, and hoist them up, as I used to see it done in San Francisco.

See cousin Cholo adjusting the noose of the great "sling-rope" round the horns of that bullock yonder. Up, up, in a moment the huge beast is suspended by his horns in mid air. Up he comes, his eyes rolling in terror. He is lowered, and laid down on the deck; instantly he springs to his feet, but another member of the Cholo family holds to the leading rope around his horns, while another seizes him by the tail, and what with pulling and pushing, and cracking the joints of the poor beast's tail, he is tied securely in his place.

I am surprised at the gentleness of these cattle. There's a Cholo walking upon the backs of a pack of them on the raft.

"Yes," replies the first mate, "they seem gentle enough now, but if you had gone into the corral where they were 'lassoed,' you would have seen them in another mood. I

2*

went one day to get a dozen choice bullocks for the ship. The owner told me to go in and make my own selection; so I walked in. They made a furious charge, and if I had not succeeded in leaping the fence they would have gored me to death."

On they come, each one suddenly "pulled up," and passing through the same experience of surprise and terror in the ascent, and of manifest relief when they feel themselves standing again on their legs. Two hundred and two beef cattle are thus stowed away as closely as they can stand.

While we are watching this scene, the new passengers from Payta have "squatted" on every foot of vacant space on the after part of the hurricane deck. Happily our sleeping space was covered by our blankets and portmanteaus, and our claim has not been "jumped;" but since the days of Noah, who ever saw the like of this scene? I have traveled with crowds of Mohammedan pilgrims in the Mediterranean, but they had left their livestock at home. Only behold how our cousins travel. Each family has its small premises on the deck. The bed is usually in the centre, surrounded by boxes, bundles and bags, on and around which are the parents, children, servants, dogs, poultry, and pets of every kind.

Next me on the "larboard" side is a huge chest. The owner sleeps on it, and, close to my pillow, he has a cock and a few hens, to wake me early in the morning. Close to our feet are two well-dressed Chinamen.

Nearly opposite, on the "starboard" side, is a quiet, seriously-disposed peacock, a beautiful creature, but apparently he does not enjoy sea life. Next to him is poor old Briggs, a broken-down cooper from a condemned whaling ship. Mr. B., as might be supposed, is from New Bedford, but has been on this coast for about thirty years. His Chileno wife and grown-up children reside in Talcahuana, and he is home-ward bound. He says he got the bishop to marry him, and paid him two hundred dollars for the job, and had, as usual in this country, to promise to be a good Roman Catholic. He would be a very tall man if he would stand erect, but what with hard work, and hard drinking, he is badly bent. He is greatly annoyed by a game-cock that persistently mounts his chest to crow. The short string that holds him will not admit of his reach-ing the cooper's bag that lies across the end of his chest, but from time to time he flies up, and by the aid of his wings, hangs upon the bag by one leg, and crows till old B.'s hard words fetch him down.

Near neighbor to Briggs is a well-dressed, patient, blind cousin of ours. He seems to be a brother of the man who sleeps upon his big box next to me. Over my head hangs a huge gourd perforated with air-holes to give ventilation to its inhabitants—a lot of very small pet birds. A few feet forward of us is a domesticated "fly up the creek," differing a little from the species of North America. He seems to view the situation calmly. Next to the water-fowl is a huge turkey-gobbler, apparently as much at home as if in a barn-yard, and quite as noisy as if he were in one. Parrots and paroquets keep up a continual chattering. Monkeys jump about and give variety to the scene. Ducks and geese sustain their parts of the music, and birds of nearly every feather contribute their notes to the harmony.

Down yonder we see a lot of huge lobsters fresh from the sea, and on that great ridge of bananas are a number of land terrapins crawling about for bodily exercise. This is life among our country cousins: such sights and sounds! It is worth a voyage from New York just to travel a week thus with our kin in their unrestrained real life, as they have it at home.

On Thursday, the 3d of November, we woke up at anchor in Callao harbor. I can truly say, as it regards wholesome fare, and improved condition of health, it was the best voyage of my life.

II.

BEFORE we enter upon the details of real life in this land, let us ascend to the summit of Chimborazo, a full view of which we had on our voyage down the coast, and, like Moses from Pizgah, take one grand view of the whole continent.

A minister in England, of my acquaintance, once made a visit to Ireland; landing at Kingstown, near the city of Dublin, he heard, among the crowd of "jaunting car" drivers, one fellow shouting in a stentorian voice, "Here, gentlemen, is the poetical horse! Here's your chance for a ride after the poetical horse!"

The minister, struck with the novelty of such a ride, soon mounted the car and was on his way toward the city, quite in advance of all the company; but soon they all drove past and left him far in the rear.

The minister, with some show of disap-

38

pointment and impatience, said to the driver: "Why do you call this lazy brute a poetical horse?"

"Sure, and he is. May it plaze your riverence, and it's yourself that can see that he is a poetical horse, for all his going is in his imagination."

Thus we shall go in imagination to the top of Chimborazo, since ascent by any other mode is impossible, and view the land where our kindred dwell.

Here we are at an elevation of 21,420 feet above the roll of the ocean; here, perpetual snow has resisted through the ages the melting heat of a tropical sun; here, by telescopic mental vision, we scan the outlines of one of the greatest continents of the globe, and get glimpses of its vast and varied resources and populations. This stupendous mountain, on whose sublime height we stand, is located near the equator, within the geographical boundaries of the Republic of Ecuador. We stand on but one of numerous towering altitudes of the Andes. There is our near neighbor, "Antisana," rising to an elevation of 19,137 feet, and her twin sister, "Cotopaxi," 18,880 feet high. This twin sister got into a dreadful paroxysm last June, and belched up through her awful throat countless millions of tons of ashes.

A merchant residing in the city of Quito told me that in that city, more than twenty miles distant, at 4 P.M. of that dismal day, the clouds of ashes so darkened the heavens that the people had to light their lamps.

"Having business down in the city," said he, "I carried my umbrella, and it caught such an accumulation of ashes that I had to lower and shake it, precisely as in a heavy fall of snow. This continued till the ground was covered with ashes four inches deep."

The twin sister had just cleared her throat; then with an awful heaving, she discharged great burning bowlders, followed by a river of lava that rushed down the sides of the mountain and consumed and swept away a number of villages, including many of the best cotton manufactories in the country. To intensify the horrors of that memorable night, the devil of revolution broke loose in the city of Quito, and the ashes were reddened with the blood of many of our unhappy cousins. As usual, the strife was between the "liberal" and the "church" parties. The liberals triumphed.

Scanning these high altitudes southwestwardly, we see two great ranges of the Andes extending southwardly through the continent from Ecuador to the Straits of Magellan. They are about a hundred miles distant from each other. The westerly range is the great backbone of the continent—a huge rampart extending from the equator to Patagonia, about four thousand miles, without a single break or pass. The rivers of the west coast are, as a matter of course, comparatively small. The vast extent of country between these two great cordilleras is covered by highland plains, lakes, detached mountains and valleys. The easterly Andes range, though one continuous chain, vying in its sublime heights with those of the west, has a number of breaks through which the rivers, fed by the heavy rains and dissolving snows of the mountains, find their way north, east, and south to the Atlantic Ocean.

Far to the northeast, we see the Orinoco, 1,500 miles in length, with its numerous tributaries, trending its way through Venezuela to the sea.

Away to the southeast we see the great river of British Guiana, the Essequibo. Di-

rectly east of us flows, not the longest, but the
largest river on the globe, fed by more than
a hundred tributaries, running from all points
of the compass. The Mississippi is about
4,000 miles in length; the Amazon is reputed
to be 3,600 miles long, but I have not seen
the man who had measured it. More accurate surveys may prove it to be much longer
than it is now supposed to be. Far down to
the southeast we behold a stream 2,250 miles
in length, which is 150 miles wide at its
mouth—Rio de la Plata, the River of Silver.

Now let us glance at the Republic of Ecuador. It extends from north latitude 1° 50′
to south latitude 40° 50′, and from 70° to 80°
west longitude. It comprises an area of 248,-
380 square miles. Its population is officially
set down at 1,308,000, of whom one half are
aboriginal tribes. I will have you understand from the beginning that I have not
surveyed these countries nor counted their
inhabitants; and therefore cannot vouch for
minute accuracy beyond an exact copy of official statistics, which may be relied upon as
sufficiently accurate for our purpose.

Our Ecuadorean cousins are reputed to
be very industrious. They cultivate the soil,

gather indigenous products of the mountains, and carry on various industries, especially the manufacture of woolen and cotton goods. But owing to excessive rains, earthquakes, volcanic eruptions, and political revolutions, their country is often devastated and its inhabitants impoverished.

Quito, the capital, has a population of fifty thousand souls. They carry on a large inland trade with their neighbors of the United States of Columbia.

Guayaquil, with a population of fifteen thousand, on the banks of the Guayas River, eighty miles up from its mouth, is the principal port of Ecuador. The Guayas is the largest river of the west coast, but is navigable for large ships only about a hundred miles.

Now adjust your glass and scan the evergreen forests of Ecuador. Away on those mountain ridges are forests of the cinchona tree, the tree that furnishes Peruvian bark, from which quinine is prepared. I have read somewhere that its medical qualities were first manifested in the cure of a lady of note in Lima, whose name was Cinchona; hence this foreign name of the tree, and the association of Peru with its bark. One of its native names is quine; hence, quinine.

Lower down, the eye rests upon the deep-green glossy foliage of the india-rubber trees. They are tapped like the sugar-maple, and the sap is boiled down to its proper consistency. This tree, however, differing from the sugar tree, bleeds to death by the tapping of one season; and but few of these, or of the cinchona, are planted to supply the waste caused by their destruction.

Upon a yet lower level down along the lesser hills and the vales, we discover cultivated orchards of the cocoanut, and the cocoa-bean trees, both of similar name, but entirely different in species.

The cocoa-bean tree is somewhat similar to the orange, but its fruit is not suspended from the small branches, as is the case with oranges and apples. The pods, about two inches in diameter, and about six in length, are red when ripe.

These pods grow out of the trunk of the tree, and from the thicker portion of the large limbs. The beans are dried and exported in sacks to Europe, where the oil is expressed for various purposes, and of the oil-cake, chocolate and cocoa are manufactured for table use. These beans pay the Ecuadorian culti-vater a better profit than any other product.

In the valleys are plantations of sugar, coffee, cotton, tobacco, a great variety of veg-etables, and the most marvelous growth of tropical fruits. It often requires two men to handle a bunch of plantains. This fruit in appearance is very much like the banana, but is quite a different kind of fruit, being edible only when baked or fried.

The mountain slopes and ravines of Ecua-dor are said to be rich in minerals—gold, sil-ver, quicksilver, lead, iron, copper, and eme-ralds; but these mines are not worked as yet with any considerable profit.

Ecuador has a revenue of about $2,000,000, and a public debt of $3,500,000. Her im-ports to Great Britain alone for 1876 amounted to $1,146,210, and her corresponding exports were $1,222,585. The government makes lib-eral appropriations for public instruction, but I am told that much time is taken in counting beads and repeating "Ave Marias," and not much solid, useful instruction imparted. Pass-ing the northern boundaries of Ecuador, glance at the UNITED STATES OF COLOMBIA, a group of nine States covering the north-western part of the continent, together with Darien, the Isthmus connecting the two continents of America. The Republic of Colombia extends from 0° 36' to 12° 25' north latitude, and from 69° 14' to 83° west longitude, comprising an area of 320,750 square miles, occupied by a population numbering 2,851,858: more than half are whites and half-castes. Three great ranges of the Andes traverse this Republic, the easterly being the largest, with a series of vast table-lands abounding in all tropical products, as also in some of those of the temperate zone. The climate is asserted to be salubrious and healthful. Most of our Colombian cousins reside on the plateaus included in an extensive cool mountain region. The inhabitants of these States hold a high rank among their South American neighbors for intelligence and culture. *The Panama Star and Herald* is one of the great journals of this newspaper age. According to authentic statistical statements, this Republic appropriates more than a million of dollars annually for public instruction; it supports 2,113 common schools, and sixty academies and colleges for higher education. Religious liberty, too, is established by law.

The annual revenue of these States is about three and a half million dollars; their national debt, ten millions. Bogota, with a population of 40,000, is the capital.

We next glance at the REPUBLIC OF VENE-ZUELA. It covers an area of 403,276 square miles, and contains a population of 1,784,194. Her annual revenue is three and a half mill-ions; her public debt, forty millions. For a small country, her exports of coffee, cocoa, sug-ar, tobacco, indigo, cinchona-bark, dye-woods, hides, tallow, timber, and metallic ores are large. Most of these products are sent to Great Britain and Europe. Her annual im-ports from England amount to over three million dollars. I recently traveled with a merchant who had resided ten years in this Republic. He told me that seven revolutions had taken place during that period, each revo-lution installing a new President. This pro-tracted struggle was between the Church and Liberal parties. The Liberal eventually tri-umphed, and drove the Jesuits out of the country. Since their exodus, during a period of seven years, the country has enjoyed peace and prosperity. God bless our Venezuelan cousins!

Easterly from Venezuela, we see British, Dutch, and French Guiana.

BRITISH GUIANA covers an area of 85,000 square miles, extending from 8° 40' to 0° 40' north of the Equator, and contains a population of 200,000 souls, of whom 1,500 are English; about 30,000 are East Indians and 10,000 Chinamen. With some small tribes of Aborigines, the remainder are of African descent.

Georgetown, in the Province of Demerara, and New Amsterdam, in the Province of Berbice, are the only towns of any note. This is a country of extensive unbroken forests, but the lowlands bordering upon the Atlantic are cultivated. The large sugar estates are bounded and subdivided by canals instead of fences; and for transporting the products of the fields boats are used instead of wagons. Causeways, formed by the soil raised in digging the canals, are made into roads for public travel. Here mangoes, plantains, bananas, oranges, cocoanuts, and other tropical fruits, and a great variety of vegetables abound.

The annual exports of British Guiana to England, consisting principally of sugar and rum, amount to about fourteen millions of dollars. I ever cherish a grateful remembrance of the kindness of my cousins during my sojourn in British Guiana about twelve years ago, and of the happy hundreds of them who received the Savior during my labors among them.

The Essequibo, a large navigable river, traverses the whole length of their country.

Now adjust your lens of a telescope for a horizontal sweep over the vast EMPIRE OF BRAZIL. Our royal cousin, His Majesty Dom Pedro, honored our Centennial Exhibition in Philadelphia with his presence.

This great country was discovered by Pedro Alvarez Cabral, a Portuguese navigator, in the year A. D. 1500.

It is bounded on the north by the Atlantic Ocean, Guiana, and Venezuela; on the west and south-west by the United States of Colombia, Ecuador, Peru, Bolivia, Paraguay, and the Argentine Republic; on the south by Uraguay; and on the east by the Atlantic Ocean. It extends from 4° 30′ north latitude, to 33° 45′ south, and from 34° 45′ to 72° 30′ west longitude. This vast domain stretches from north to south a distance of two thousand six hundred miles, and two thousand five

3

hundred miles from the Atlantic to the Andes, covering an area of 3,288,000 square miles. Many Yankees entertain the idea that we possess the largest country on the globe. We do not say that our people are not, in some respects, the most extraordinary people on the globe; but, be that as it may, here are some figures to be considered.

The United States covers an area of 3,026,094 square miles, not including Alaska, which contains 1,539,706 square miles, and a fractional squatter's claim of 160 acres. Hence, the domain of the Empire of Brazil is 261,906 square miles larger than the domain of the United States of North America.

The population of Brazil is put down at 10,200,000—a little less than one-fourth of the population of the United States. One million and a half of these were slaves, but, by a law passed on September 28th, 1871, providing for gradual emancipation, their bonds have been broken, and a few years hence there will not be a slave in the realm. Half a million are Indians. There are fifty German colonies, containing 40,000 Germans, and quite a sprinkling of English and Scotch; but the great bulk of the population are of Portuguese descent and mixed blood. The Portuguese language is the common vernacular of the people of Brazil.

The army consists of 16,600 men, enlisted voluntarily. The navy includes fifty-four vessels; eleven of them are iron-clads, and seven are monitors. The Empire is divided into twenty Provinces, and certain territories. It possesses unequaled facilities, in the number and size of its rivers, for interior navigation, and has about 2,000 miles of railroads in running order.

The lowlands abound in all tropical productions. The table-lands, at the elevation of from three to five thousand feet, produce plentifully of the temperate-zone cereals and fruits.

The mineral resources of Brazil are believed to be good, but have not yet been extensively explored.

The revenue of Brazil for 1876 was upward of $58,000,000.

In common with other countries, great and small, she has a heavy national debt, amounting to about $300,000,000.

Her annual imports from and exports to England alone amount respectively to about $30,000,000.

May the gracious God of Nations cause His
face to shine on Dom Pedro II. and on his
people! Amen!

Now pause a moment to contemplate the
spunky little REPUBLIC OF PARAGUAY. It is
sandwiched between Brazil and the Argentine
Republic, yet it has an interesting history of
its own. It was under the dominion of the
Jesuits for two hundred years. Finally, in
1768, the people rose and expelled them from
their borders. Later, in 1811, they broke off
the Spanish yoke, and became an independent
nation.

Their territory comprises an area of 56,700
square miles, occupied by 300,000 people.
Their annual government revenue amounts to
about $600,000. Our Paraguayan cousins are
entitled to our confidence and love. The Lord
bless them!

Still farther on, beyond the southern boun-
dary of the great Brazilian Empire, is the little
REPUBLIC OF URUGUAY. A river bearing its
own name bounds it on the west, with the
Rio de La Plata and the Atlantic on the south
and east.

Our Uruguan cousins obtained their independence in 1825. They own 70,000 square

miles of land, maintain a population of 550,000, and have an annual revenue of six and a half million dollars. England sells them every year about $5,000,000 worth of her manufactures, and buys of them about $4,000,000 worth of their products, these consisting largely of wool, hides, hams, and tallow.

We will now glance at the vast country of our Argentine cousins, numbering about 2,000,000. Their country, the ARGENTINE REPUBLIC, extends from 22° to 41° south latitude, and contains 838,600 square miles. Besides, they claim all that portion of Patagonia east of the Andes, adding 376,000 square miles to their domain, and 24,000 Indians to their population. Buenos Ayres is their great emporium. Thirteen lines of steamers ply between that city and Europe, whence an immense immigration, especially from Italy, is continually pouring into the Republic. Our cousins there are an enterprising people, and, besides a heavy export of raw materials common to South America, they export, annually, in wrought and unwrought iron to the value of $3,125,000; woolen manufactures, over $2,000,000; cotton goods, over $4,500,000; apparel and haberdashery, $1,400,000; hardware and cutlery, nearly $1,000,000; leather, saddlery, and harness, over $800,000. They have about 1,000 miles of railroads. Well done, ye thrifty Argentine cousins.

The REPUBLIC OF CHILE next demands our attention. The grandest mountain of the whole Andes range is in Chile, the Acancagua, which rises to an elevation of 23,100 feet above the ocean. Its summit would be a better stand-point for our present view, but we will not be at the trouble to change our base. Chile lies between the great west chain of the Andes and the ocean, a well-watered, fertile country, about one hundred miles in width. As Argentina claims all of Patagonia east of the Andes, so Chile claims all of that dreary region west of the Andes.

The domain of Chile, therefore, extends from Bolivia to Cape Horn—from latitude 20° to 50° south, a stretch of 2,200 miles. Chile is divided into sixteen Provinces, and has a geographical area of 126,060 square miles. According to the statistical pamphlet they presented at the Centennial Exhibition in Philadelphia, their population reaches 2,319,266. The annual revenue of Chile is about $16,-000,000; her national debt, about $50,000,-

000. Her foreign imports for 1876 were $35,-291,041. Her exports to foreign countries for the same year were $37,771,139. She has in operation 865 miles of railway, of which 465 miles belong to the government, and the remaining 400 miles to private companies. So says my friend, John Slater, Esq., and he is one of the principal builders of the Chilean railroads.

Hereafter I shall have more to say about our Chilean cousins and their grand country. We will now give a passing glance at the REPUBLIC OF PERU. It is divided into nineteen Provinces, covers an area of 503,380 square miles, extending from latitude 3° to 22° 10′ south, and contains a population of 2,699,000, of whom 1,365,000 are males, 1,335,000 are females. It is affirmed by those who have made this a matter of observation and study that about two-thirds of the people of Peru are Indians; of the remaining one-third 60,000 are Chinese, 17,000 Italians, 2,500 English, 3,000 Germans, 2,200 French, and 600 North Americans.

The western range of the Andes traverses the Republic of Peru through its entire length of 1,300 miles, about sixty miles distant from the coast and parallel with it. The whole region looks like a great desert, except where it

is crossed by the little rivers from the mountains. With sufficient water the soil is wonderfully productive. For example, the Valley
of Chincama, north of Lima, exported sugar
last year to the value of 14,400,000 hard dollars. Some single estates yield eight thousand dollars' worth of sugar per day. The
climate is so equable that they can cut and
crush the sugar-cane during every month in
the year. These estates are owned principally by our Peruvian cousins, and worked
by Chinese coolies.

The valley in which these estates are located is connected by about 60 miles of railway with the port of Salaverry. The city of
Trujillo, with a population of 15,000, is six
miles inland from the port. Back of this valley, near the mountains, is a large deposit of
good anthracite coal. The mountain valleys
east, and much of the country of Peru lying
between the great Andes ranges, are very fertile in all tropical cereals, fruits, and vegetables. Peru is rich in silver and copper mines,
but her great source of available wealth is
in her deposits of guano and saltpeter. Her
Henry Meiggs's railroads are the greatest wonders of the world in railway engineering.

Peru has an annual revenue of about $30,-000,000, with an expenditure exceeding that sum, and a burden of over $200,000,000 of debt to carry.   Her paper currency has shrunk to half its nominal value.   The great trouble with Peru has been that the government was so rich that a large proportion of the upper classes, instead of developing the resources of the country by personal industry, quartered themselves on the government, and demanded a carte blanche on the public treasury.

When this was denied them by the party in power, the next thing was to raise a revolution, put the rulers out, and put themselves in.   Now that the treasury is empty, and the national credit at a great discount in the money markets of the world, it is to be hoped that peace will prevail, and that personal industry will develop a principle of self-reliance, and will secure adequate means of subsistence for our upper-class cousins.   I believe the country will recover her credit, and prosper, and be all the wiser for her hard experience.

Peru has 600 miles of railroads in operation, all, except two short bits of road, owned by the government.   Altogether they have drained

3*

the exchequer of $135,000,000.   More here-
after about this interesting country.

We must descend from the snowy heights
of Chimborazo before we freeze to death, but
ere we depart we must pause a moment to see
the home of our Bolivian cousins.

The REPUBLIC of BOLIVIA was called after
its Washington, Simon Bolivar.   It extends
from 9° to 26° 15′ south latitude, and contains
500,870 square miles of mountains and valleys with about 200 miles of coast on the Pacific.   Along this coast line she has four ports,
but most of her transportation is through
Peruvian ports.   Her hardy mountaineer sons
and daughters of toil, cousins of ours, count
up to the number of two millions.

Her exports consist largely of the wool of
her flocks of alapaca, llama, vicuña and sheep:
also of cinchona-bark, medical herbs, silver
and copper.   She has a revenue of about two
and three-quarter million dollars, with a debt of
ten millions.

Her army consists, according to printed
statements, of 1,100 officers, and 3,000 privates.
Her capital and largest city is La Paz, with a
population of 77,000.

I know you must be weary; but stay a

moment while I give you one or two grand summary facts to ponder at your leisure. These South American nations sum up a total population of over 26,000,000. Add to this the populations of Central America and Mexico, and we shall find the grand total to be about 38,000,000 of the Latin and mixed races, nearly all speaking one common language,—our cousins and next-door neighbors. Should we not love them, and endeavor by every possible means to do them good ?

III.

The Empire of the Incas embraced the country now occupied by Peru, Bolivia, and Ecuador. Its population is estimated to have been about 12,000,000, double the number of people now residing within the same geographical boundaries. The only historic records of the Incas of any date prior to the Spanish conquest of their country in 1550, are the relics and monuments of their own industry and mechanical skill, still found among the ruins of their ancient homes. From historic data of this sort many volumes have been written. Perhaps the best work on the subject is the very elaborate book by E. George Squier, M.A., F.S.A., published by the Harper Brothers. That is the book for the student of this ancient extinct empire; but I will give a few extracts from it, to convey some general idea of its construction and civilization.

The Inca nation proper developed in the Andes region, from Lake Titicaca to Cusco, their capital. In course of time they conquered and absorbed the great Chimu nation, and other tribes, dwelling in the valleys and plains along the Pacific coast. The Chimu were great builders of adobe palaces and towers; the Incas were wonderfully skilled in stone masonry. I will give but a few descriptive examples from the pen of Mr. Squier. About 10° south latitude, in what is now North Peru, in a beautiful valley, six miles wide and fifteen miles long, watered by the river Moche, is the ancient capital of our old cousin Chimu. "The city now consists of a wilderness of walls, forming great inclosures, each containing a labyrinth of ruined dwellings and other edifices. On one side of the city is a heavy wall, several miles of which are still standing. From this wall, extending inward at right angles, are other walls of scarcely inferior elevation, inclosing great areas which have never been built upon, and which fall off in low terraces carefully cleared of stones, each with its aqueducts for irrigation." These were doubtless the gardens and pleasure-grounds of our old Chimu cousins. Outside the wall are two rect-

angular inclosures, situated about a quarter of
a mile apart, each containing a truncated pyramid. The first of these inclosures is 252 feet
long by 222 feet wide. The remains of the
wall are 14 feet high and 6 feet thick. The
pyramid is 162 feet square, and 50 feet in
height. It is built, as are the walls, of compact
rubble, or tenacious clay mixed with broken
stones so as to form a solid, enduring mass.
This appears to have been the burying-place
for girls from five to fifteen years of age. The
other pyramid is 240 feet long by 210 feet
wide. The outer walls are 20 feet high and 8
feet thick, with an inner mound 172 feet long
by 152 feet wide, and 40 feet high. There is
in this city a reservoir 450 feet long by 195
feet in width, and 60 feet deep, with terraced
steps of clean-cut stones extending down to
the bottom. Cousin Chimu built another pyramid in this neighborhood called the Temple
of the Sun, which was over 800 feet long, 470
feet wide, covering an area of over seven acres.
The greatest height of this terraced structure
is upward of 200 feet. It is built of huge
adobes.

The Chimu family were not only great builders, but skillful workers in gold, silver, and cop-

per, especially in ornamental imitations of fish, lizards, snakes, and birds. They also made agricultural instruments in bronze, together with knives, trowels, etc. They excelled in the manufacture of pottery, and could make as fine cotton goods as are woven in Manchester or New England looms of to-day. Mr. Squier examined a piece in which he "counted 62 threads of warp and woof to the inch. The finest Egyptian mummy cloth has but 44 threads to the inch."

Mr. Squier gives an account of the Mecca of the Chimu. Here are a few illustrative paragraphs:

The *Ruins of Pachacamac*, on the banks of the river Lurin, are situated on a high bluff overlooking the sea, twenty miles south of the city of Lima. Pachacamac was the chief divinity of our ancient Peruvian cousins. "The name signifies, 'He who animates the universe' —'the Creator of the world.'" A chronicler of Pizzaro, named Estete, gives the following account of the idol bearing this great name, and of the place he occupied. "The idol was in a good house, well painted and finished. In one room, closely shut, very dark and stinking, was the idol, made of wood, very dirty, which

they call god, who creates and sustains all
things. At his feet were some offerings of
golden ornaments. He is held in such high
veneration, that none except his priests and
servants, whom it is supposed he has elected,
may enter his presence, or touch the walls of
the house. He is held throughout the country
as god, and to this idol they make great sacri-
fices: and pilgrims from a distance of nine
hundred miles and more bring offerings of
gold, silver, and clothing. These they give to
the custodian, who enters and consults the
idol, and returns with his answer. All the
people from a great distance who come every
year to pay tribute to this temple have houses
in which to place their offerings."

"This town of Pachacamac," continues Estete, "is a great thing; alongside of the temple
is a house on a hill, well built, with five inclosures or walls, which the Indians say is
the sun"—probably dedicated to sun worship.
"There are also in the town many other large
houses, with terraces like those of Spain. It
must be a very old place, for there are numerous fallen edifices. It has been surrounded by
a wall, although now most of it is fallen. It
has large gates for entering, and also streets."

At the time this description was penned, the Spaniards took away from this temple of Pachacamac sixteen hundred and eighty-seven pounds' weight of gold, and sixteen thousand ounces of silver. The great body of the treasure, amounting, it was said, to twenty-five thousand pounds' weight of gold and silver, had been hid somewhere between Lurin and Lima. The following incident gives some idea of the wealth of this temple, before it was despoiled. "A pilot of Pizzaro asked for the silver nails and tacks which had supported the plates of silver, bearing the sacred name of their god, on the walls of the temple, as his share of the spoils, which Pizzaro granted, as a trifling thing, but which amounted to more than thirty-two thousand ounces." The Incas had long before conquered and taken the city and people of Pachacamac, but instead of destroying and superseding their temple and worship, they simply subsidized it by building one of their own alongside of it.

A FAMILY TOMB of our old cousins in the city of Pachacamac was opened, and thus described by Mr. Squier: "This tomb, walled with adobes"—sun-dried bricks—"was four feet square, by three feet deep, and contained five bodies: one of a man of middle age; another of a full-grown woman; a third of a girl of about fourteen years; the fourth of a boy about seven; and the fifth an infant." The dear little cousin "was placed between the father and the mother; the boy was by the side of the man; and the girl was by the side of the woman. All were enveloped in a braided network, or sack of rushes, or coarse grass, bound closely around the bodies by cords of the same material.

"Under the outer wrapper of braided reeds around the man, was another of stout, plain cotton cloth, fastened with a variegated cord of llama wool. Next came the envelope of cotton cloth of finer texture, which, when removed, disclosed the body shrunken and dried hard, of the color of mahogany, but well preserved. The hair was long and slightly reddish, perhaps from the effect of the nitre in the soil. Passing around the neck, and carefully folded on the knees, on which the head rested, was a net of the twisted fiber of the ajave, a plant not found on the coast. The threads were as fine as the finest used by our fishermen, and the meshes were neatly knotted, precisely after the fashion of to-day.

"Wrapped up in a cloth beneath his feet were some fishing-lines of various sizes, and some copper hooks, barbed like ours, and some copper sinkers," so it is evident that our old cousin was, like Simon Peter, a fisherman.

"Under each armpit was a roll of white alpaca wool, and behind the calf of each leg a few thick short ears of variegated maize, or Indian corn. A small thin piece of copper had been placed in the mouth, corresponding perhaps with the *óblos* which the ancient Greeks put into the mouths of their dead as a fee for Charon; and suspended by a thread around the neck was a pair of bronze tweezers, probably for plucking out the beard.

"The wife, beneath the same coarse outer-wrapping of braided reeds, was enveloped in a blanket of alpaca wool, finely spun, woven in a style known as 'three-ply,' in two colors— a soft chestnut-brown and pure white. Below this was a sheet of fine cotton cloth, with sixty-two threads of warp and woof to the inch.

"It had a diamond-shaped pattern, formed by very elaborate lines of ornament, inside of which, or in the spaces themselves, were representations of monkeys, which seemed to be following each other as up and down stairs. Beneath this was a rather coarsely woven, but yet soft and flexible cotton cloth, twenty yards or more in length, wrapped in many folds around the body of the woman, which was in a similar condition, as regards preservation, to that of her husband.

"Her long hair was less changed by the salts of the soil than that of her husband, and was black, and in most places lustrous. In one hand she held a comb, made by setting what I took to be the bony parts—the rays of fishes' fins—in a slip of the hard woody part of the dwarf palm-tree, into which they were not only tightly cemented, but firmly bound.

"In her other hand were the remains of a fan with a cane handle, from the upper points of which radiated the faded feathers of parrots and humming-birds. Around her neck was a triple necklace of shells, dim in color and exfoliating layer after layer when exposed to light and air. Resting between her body and bent-up knees were several small domestic implements, among them an ancient spindle for spinning cotton, half covered with spun thread, which connected with a mass of the raw cotton. This simple spinning apparatus consisted of a section of the stalk of the quinoa, half as large as the little finger, and eight inches long, its lower end fitted through a whirl-bob of stone to give it momentum when set in motion by a twirl of the forefinger and thumb, grasping a point of hard wood stuck in the upper end of the spindle. The contrivance is precisely the same as that in universal use by the Indian women of the present day. One of the most interesting articles found with the woman was a kind of wallet, composed of two pieces of thick cotton cloth of different colors, ten inches long by five broad, the lower end of each terminating in a fringe, and the upper end of each corner in a long braid, the braids of both being again braided together. These cloths placed together were carefully folded up and tied by the braids. The pocket contained some 'Lima beans,' a few pods of cotton gathered before maturity, the husks being still on, some fragments of an ornament of thin silver, and two little thin disks of the same material, three-tenths of an inch in diameter, and pierced with a small hole near its edge, too minute for ornament apparently, and possibly used as a coin; also tiny beads of chalcedony, scarcely an eighth of an inch in diameter.

"The body of the girl was in a peculiar position, having been seated on a kind of work-box of braided reeds, with a cover hinged on one side, and shutting down and fastening on the other. It was about eighteen inches long, fourteen wide, and eight deep, and contained a greater variety of articles than I ever found together in any grave of the aborigines. There were grouped together things childish, and things showing approach to maturity. There were rude specimens of knitting, with places showing where stitches had been dropped; mites of spindles and implements for weaving, and braids of thread of irregular thickness, kept as if for sake of contrast with others larger and nicely wound with a finer and more even thread. There were skeins and spools of thread; the spools being composed of two splints placed across each other at right angles, and the thread wound in and out between them. There were strips of cloth, some wide, some narrow, and some of two and even three colors. There were pouches plain and variegated, of different sizes, and all woven or knit without a seam. There were needles of bone and of bronze; a comb and a little bronze knife, and some other articles; a fan, smaller than that of the mother, was also stored away in the box. There were several sections of the hollow bones of some bird, carefully stopped by a wad of cotton, and containing pigments of various colors. With these I found a curious contrivance made of the finest cotton, evidently used as a 'dob' for applying the colors to the face.

"By the side of these novel cosmetic boxes was a contrivance for rubbing or grinding the pigments to the requisite fineness for use. It was a small oblong stone, with a cup-shaped hollow on the upper side, in which fits a little round stone ball answering the purpose of a pestle. There was also a substitute for a mirror, composed of a piece of iron pyrites, resembling the half of an egg, with the plain side highly polished. Among all these many curious things was a little crushed ornament of gold, evidently intended to represent a butterfly, but so thin and delicate that it came to pieces and lost its form when we attempted to handle it.

"There was also a netting instrument of hard

wood, not unlike those now in use in making nets.

"The envelopes of the girl were similar to those that enshrouded her mother. Her hair was braided and plaited around the forehead, encircling which, also, was a cincture of white cloth, ornamented with little silver spangles; a thin narrow bracelet of the same metal still hung on the shrunken arm, and between her feet was the dried body of a parrot, doubtless her pet in life, brought perhaps from the distant Amazonian valleys.

"There was nothing of special interest surrounding the body of the boy; but bound tightly around his forehead was his sling, finely braided with cotton threads." The dear little fellow, that was all his stock in trade.

"The body of the infant, a girl, had been imbedded in the fleece of the alpaca, then wrapped in fine cotton cloth, and placed in a strongly braided sack of rushes, with handles or loops at each end as if for carrying it. The only article found with this body was a sea-shell containing pebbles, the orifice closed with a hard pitch-like substance." That was our baby cousin's rattle.

"Besides the bodies there were a number of utensils and other articles in the vault; among them half a dozen earthen jars, pans and pots of various sizes and ordinary form. One or two were still incrusted with the soot of the fires over which they had been used. Every one contained something. One was filled with peanuts, another with maize, etc.; and there were some others representing the religious notions of the occupants of the tomb."

INCA ARCHITECTURE.

Mr. Squier, speaking of the Inca architecture of Cuzco, the capital of the Inca empire, says:

"Some of these walls are massive and imposing, composed of hard and heavy stones. Those sustaining the terrace of the Palace of the Inca Rocco, in the street of Triunfo, are of a compact, fine-grained sienite, some of them weighing several tons each, and fitted together with wonderful precision.

"The remains of the palaces and temples of Cuzco enable us, with the aid of the early descriptions, to make out with tolerable accuracy their original form and character.

"As a rule, they were built around a court,

4

presenting exteriorly an unbroken wall, having but a single entrance, and, except in rare instances, no exterior windows. The entrance in all cases was broad and lofty, permitting a horseman to ride in without difficulty. The lintel was always a heavy slab of stone, sometimes carved, as well as the jambs, with figures, those of serpents predominating. These entrances were closed by heavy doors.

"The walls of these structures, as well as those supporting the terraces, inclined slightly inward, and in some instances are narrowed somewhat near the top. Those of Cuzco are all of cut stone of brown trachyte, the grain of which being rough, causes greater adhesion between the blocks than would be effected by the use of other kinds of stone.

"The stones of some structures range in length from one to eight feet, and in thickness from six inches to two feet. They are laid in regular courses, the larger stones generally at the bottom, each course diminishing in thickness toward the top of the wall, thus giving a very pleasant effect of graduation. The joints are all of a precision unknown in our architecture, and not rivaled in the remains of ancient art that had fallen under my notice in Europe.

The statement of old writers, that the accuracy with which the stones of some structures were fitted together was such that it was impossible to introduce the thinest knife-blade or finest needle between them, may be taken as strictly true. The world has nothing to show in the way of stone-cutting to surpass the skill and accuracy displayed in the Inca structures of Cuzco.

"In the buildings I am describing there is absolutely no cement of any kind, nor the remotest evidence of any having been used. The Inca architects depended, with rare exceptions, on the accuracy of their stone fitting without cement for the stability of their works —works which, unless disturbed by systematic violence, will endure until the Capitol at Washington has sunk into decay, and Macaulay's New-Zealander contemplates the ruins of St. Paul's from the crumbling arches of London Bridge.

"Nearly all* the rooms of an Inca house opened from the court. As a rule these had no connection, and seem to have been dedicated each to a special purpose. In some cases, nevertheless, there were inner chambers, to be reached only after passing through a number

of outer ones. These were, perhaps, recesses
sacred to domestic or religious rites, or places
of refuge for the timid or weak. Many of the
apartments were large. Garcilasso de la Vega
describes some of them, of which the remains
exist to indicate his accuracy, as capable of receiving sixty horsemen with room enough to
exercise with their lances. Three sides of the
great central square were occupied by as many
grand public edifices, in which religious and
other ceremonies were observed in bad weather,
each of which had the capacity to receive
several thousand people. Some of them indeed are two hundred paces long, and from fifty
to sixty broad, and capable of holding 3,000
people each.

"Prescott and others have fallen into the
error of describing all the buildings of the
ancient Peruvians as of only a single story,
low, and without windows. Now, the walls
which remain, show that in Cuzco they were
from thirty-five to forty feet high, besides the
spring of the roof. They were perhaps all of
a single story, but elsewhere we know there
were edifices, private dwellings as well as
temples, of two and three stories, with windows
adequate for all purposes of illuminating their

interiors; regard being had to the temperature of the country, which with a people unacquainted with glass, would limit the number of apertures to absolute requirements."

"The second Temple of the Sun in Cuzco is 800 feet long, and 200 feet broad." Mr. Squier measured blocks of polished porphyry, in the walls of an Inca fortress, eighteen feet long, five feet broad, and four feet thick; and others, twenty-one feet long and fifteen feet broad, and five feet thick, and so perfectly fitted together that it was almost impossible to find the joints.

Old Cousin Chimu, Cousin Inca, and all their large families, like the Hindūs, had gods innumerable. There were three principal classes: village gods, household gods, and personal gods. Padré Arriaga gives the following description of the fervid character of their worship:

"The various families came carrying the dried bodies of their ancestors, together with those taken from the churches, as if the living and the dead were coming to judgment. Also the higher and lower priests, dressed in their robes and plumes, with the offerings for the gods in pots, jars, and vases, with copper and silver trumpets, and large sea-shells, on which they blow to convene the people, who came with tambourines, well made, hardly a woman being without one, bringing also a great number of *cunas*, a kind of cradle with carved sides, and figure-head of some animal which was an object of worship."

The manner of converting our cousins from the error of their ways is described by the same Padré in an account of his first visit to the northern provinces in 1618. He states that he "confessed 6,794 persons; detected 679 ministers of idolatry, and made them do penance." He enumerates the number and variety of the gods he destroyed, making altogether 5,676 objects of idolatrous worship. Besides all this he adds that he "chastised seventy-three witches."

What a great revivalist was Padré Arriaga! According to the historic narrative, the Spaniards long before this pious raid upon our cousins, had killed 40,000 of them in that region. I suppose the natives had a good deal of the old Adam in them, and were rather hard to convert.

"And were they indeed descendants of Adam?"

It is written, "Adam begot a son in his own likeness," and so the family likeness passed down through the generations. The ancient Incas had, and their progeny of to-day have all the properties, proportions, and features of the Adamic family.

"How did they get to South America?" Now, instead of troubling ourselves with dubious second-hand speculations on this subject, let us accept God's foundation facts as our data in the premises, and draw our conclusions accordingly. Read the record of man's creation and chartered rights to this planet, embracing all its continents, and seas, and resources— "And God said, Let us make man in our image, after our likeness: and let them have dominion over the fish of the sea, and over the fowl of the air, and over the cattle, and over all the earth, and over every creeping thing that creepeth upon the earth. So God created man in His own image, in the image of God created He him; male and female created He them. And God blessed them, and God said unto them, Be fruitful, and multiply, and replenish the earth, and subdue it: and have dominion over the fish of the sea, and over the fowl of the air, and over every living thing that moveth upon the earth. And God said, Behold I have given you every herb bearing seed, which is upon the face of all the earth, and every tree, in the which is the fruit of a tree yielding seed: to you it shall be for meat. And to every beast of the earth, and to every fowl of the air, and to every thing that creepeth upon the earth, wherein there is life, I have given every green herb for meat, and it was so. And God saw every thing that he had made, and behold it was very good."—GEN. I. 26–31.

Every fruitful mountain and hill is a monumental attestation of the Divine authority of this record. Every body of water, whether flowing in rivers or swayed in ocean's depths in perpetual ebb and flood by a lunar touch of God, and the millions of creatures that daily get their food from God, attest the genuineness of the charter it contains. Every living thing in air, earth, or sea owes its existence to the primal provisions and continued force of these chartered rights of Adam and his posterity. Imagine with Darwin, if you choose, that in the dusky ages of antiquity some enterprising old monkey doffed his tail and straightened out his hind legs, and a female of the same tribe, with such an illustrious example before her eyes, went through the same remarkable transformation, and the pair of them became the progenitors of a race of intellectual bipeds. But if this transformation could have taken place, the newcomers could not obtain from the king of the country even a squatter's right to a foot of land, nor a single source of subsistence, without a change of this grand old charter.

It must be admitted that Adam's revolt from God has occasioned a great change in the Divine administration of government over this world; but the fact of man's continued existence in it, and the continuance of all the resources enumerated so specifically in our bill of chartered rights, go to demonstrate beyond a doubt: 1st, that God has not abdicated his government over this colonial outpost of His great empire; 2d, that He has not ignored this ancient charter of human rights; 3d, that, perverted as we are, He entertains a purpose of love and mercy concerning us—at least commensurate with His great outlay of natural resources on our behalf. True, the King of this world in His moral administration, exercises His right, directly or by any agency available, both in regard to individuals and nations, to abase or to exalt whom He will; yet this grand

4*

charter of human rights, and the vital resources it includes, remain unchanged.

But "how did the Incas get across the great Pacific Ocean into South America"?

Did we not read in the charter that man "was made in the image and after the likeness of God"? Would not such godlike powers of intellect be adequate to the full measure of his responsibility? Did not God give the planet, with its earth and seas, to him, and command him to replenish it and subdue it? Would God give and order without also furnishing every resource requisite to its execution?

This is the fact in the case. Before the nations descending from Noah sank down so deeply into the slime-pits of lust and idolatry as to preclude the exercise of their genius and capacity for bold adventure, they crossed the waters and took possession of every part of the habitable earth, "to replenish and subdue" it, according to the commandment of their Creator. Christopher Columbus, as a discoverer, was as one born out of due time. Every country in the world had been discovered and colonized long before he was born; so long that their charts and log-books had all

been lost—lost, indeed, before history began;
but their colonies, still remaining to this day,
demonstrate the maritime skill and bold adventure of the men who planted them. With
the model of Noah's great ship, more commodious than the "Great Eastern," why should
they not build ships, and navigate the seas in
those days?

Though the decree, as a part of the penalty
entailed by sin, was pronounced upon man,
"Dust thou art, and unto dust shalt thou return," yet his body, unmarred by the effects of
abuse and hereditary ills, possessed such stamina and vitality, as to resist the wear and waste
of nearly a thousand years. So, many nations, under the teaching of God's prophets,
from the days of Noah till the days Job, retained a vast amount of moral stamina, and
acquired such knowledge of the principles of
government, science, social institutions, and
civilization generally, as to survive the storms
of centuries, after they had lost the knowledge
of God. The history of their apostasy is
graphically stated by St. Paul—"When they
knew God, they glorified Him not as God,
neither were thankful; but became vain in
their imaginations, and their foolish heart

was darkened. Professing themselves to be wise, they became fools, and changed the glory of the uncorruptible God into an image made like to corruptible man, and to birds, and four-footed beasts, and creeping things. Wherefore, God also gave them up to uncleanness through the lusts of their own hearts, to dishonor their own bodies, and to a reprobate mind." Such elements of corruption and of disintegration must end in utter debasement and ruin; but the salt, or conserving power of the few men who fear God and work righteousness in every nation, and of a few sound principles of truth, give an astonishing vital cohesive force for the preservation of the civilized nations of antiquity.

The facts of history, such as the perfection of the languages spoken by heathen nations, the vestiges of ancient science and architecture found among them, go to prove that the further we trace their history back along their ancestral lines toward Noah, who had the knowledge of the true God, the greater was their power of genius and achievement; thence, the further down the stream of heathenism they drift, the greater their demoralization and imbecility.

At the great Centennial in Philadelphia, where the best artistic skill of civilized heathen nations was exhibited, it was plainly manifest that in the manufacture of pottery, and various articles in bronze, silver, gold, and ivory, things more ornamental than useful, and in the manufacture of silks, etc., they displayed great imitative skill; but as for remaining genius to invent anything new, or of moral power to get out of their old grooves, there was no evidence of either; hence, but for the emancipating power of the Gospel, enfranchising nations once in the chains of barbarous heathenism, there would not to-day be a steam-engine in the world, nor a labor-saving machine of any sort.

Ancient science, art, and civilization flourished most in the great centers of population. The adventurers who struck out new lines of discovery, and opened up new countries for settlement, would have but a very limited knowledge of the higher education of their own advanced men, and their children born in remote regions would know still less, but they could readily retain and transmit some knowledge of mechanical arts. Thus the pioneers of Asiatic emigration to North America stood much in the same relation to their cultivated Oriental contemporaries as our own Rocky Mountain trappers bear to the cultivated classes of the great literary centers of our population. The Asiatics who settled Mexico and South America, evidently came from civilized circles near to the centers and capitals of their nations. They brought with them a knowledge of civil government, architecture, and various useful arts, and yet they were not near enough to the centers of education to secure and transplant into the New World the knowledge of letters and of the sciences then known in the civilizations they had left behind.

The architecture of the Incas is simply an importation of Asiatic architecture, the magnificent ruins of which are seen in all Asiatic countries to-day.

The hardy adventurers who penetrated the forests and traversed the swamps of Europe, and laid the foundations of its empires, had no such knowledge of mechanical arts and of civilization as the Incas. They were debased idolaters and barbarians; but God's messengers, first from Palestine and Asia Minor, came to them with Gospel tidings, and the Inspired Scriptures, revealing to them the Lord Jesus, the

Divine Emancipator of individual men, and of nations; and though their reception of Him was not so cordial and unanimous as it should have been, yet they struck for liberty, and, to a large extent, gained it.

Their development of religious and intellectual freedom was imperiled, and almost defeated, by a great apostasy and compromise with heathenism; and many of the Christian nations of Europe are still involved in heathenish complications.

It was a nation possessing this mixed or partial Christianity that conquered the Incas. They had been but partially recovered from a depth of barbarous idolatry that the Incas had never reached. The Incas, to be sure, spiritually, were equally dark, but still retained much of their ancestral civilization, the like of which the European heathens had never possessed; but the light of God had shone upon the Spaniard, and hence, compared with his former self, or with any purely heathen people, he had become a man of might, with power to break down, but not with power to build up; power to destroy, but not to heal.

The Anglo-Saxons, more than any other people of the modern era, have acknowledged and received the Lord Jesus, the only Saviour of men. They willingly promote a free circulation of His Bible at home and abroad, in all lands. In proportion as they have identified themselves with Him, and His purpose and plan of bringing back all the apostate nations, kindreds, and tongues to God, He has identified Himself with them. He has given into their hands more than half of the territory of the globe, together with the command of all the seas.

What an ancient king said to his son is true in all ages of individuals and of nations—" My son, know thou the God of thy fathers, and serve Him with a perfect heart, and with a willing mind. If thou seek Him, He will be found of thee, but if thou forsake Him, He will cast thee off forever."

IV.

CALLAO is the port, with a population of about 30,000; Lima, the capital, contains a population of 120,000. The two cities are seven miles apart, connected by two railroads. After a delightful voyage of eighteen days from New York, we arrived in Callao, November 3, 1877. We land on a splendid concrete mole, 984 by 802 feet, the construction of which is reputed to have cost the French Government over $8,000,000.

"What, the French?"

Yes; in their attempts to get a footing in America some years ago, they put a line of steamers on this coast, and built these substantial piers, and own them now, though their steamers "hauled off" long ago. The work was done by English mechanics, and is utilized principally by English shipping. Near by, on the site of old Callao, a fine city, destroyed by a tidal wave over a hundred years ago, is "the

89

factory" of the P. S. N. Co., with all the great
shops and machinery required by such a company, employing four hundred men, about one
hundred of whom are English and Scotch mechanics.

Between the company's works and the city
of Callao is the immense fortress, which cost
the Spanish Government thirty millions of dollars. It is now used in part as a barracks, but
more as a custom-house and bonded warehouse.
We put up at the Commercial Hotel, but
were soon taken in charge by two kind gentlemen, and conducted to comfortable rooms provided for us in Washington Street. Many of
the streets are wide, laid smooth and solid
with "Oroya cement," and, differing from
most tropical towns I have seen, they are
as clean as they can be swept with a broom.
Nothing is allowed to be thrown on the streets,
not so much as an envelope. No system of
sewerage, but scavenger carts daily remove all
slops and nuisance from the dwellings of our
Callao cousins. How strange the houses appear! Whole blocks of one and of two story
buildings, apparently unfinished; no gables,
but all flat on the top, covered with earth;
some simply with bamboo splits. The build-

ings have a substantial appearance, painted in varied bright colors, and some of them beautiful to behold; but a large proportion of them, both here and in Lima, are constructed of "wattle and daub," or, except timber to support the structure, the walls are made of a small tough species of bamboo, plastered with a mortar made of clay, straw, and cow-dung. One India rain of forty-four hours, such as I have often seen, would leave nothing of these cities but canebrakes, mud-holes, and mounds; but this is the country in which the rains descend not, and the floods never come. Nearly all the houses of this city, and I may say of all South American cities, except the English structures of Valparaiso, are built on the Oriental plan. We enter a court by a door, or more frequently by a gateway, through which you may drive a two-horse carriage. The court is the center of the dwelling-place; from each side of the entrance-way, and on all sides of the inner square, is a continuous veranda facing the court. The doors of nearly all the apartments open directly on to the veranda. Whether the house has one or two stories the plan is the same, above and below, with stairways leading to the upper veranda. The court, in some cases, has a fountain and tank, generally a flower garden, with orange trees and other varieties of fruit. At night the court gate is shut, and the whole premises are in the main secure. The outside walls are solid, except the break of small windows, to admit light and air; they are all fortified by iron bars, like the windows of a jail, so that here "every man's house is his castle," in which he must be ready to stand for his life, or the lives of his family, against the attack of thieves who may attempt to "break through and steal," or revolutionists, who may come to contest his rights to property or life.

Lima is said to cover fourteen millions of square yards of ground. About one-half of this area is covered by private dwellings, the other half by public buildings, churches, public squares, with botanical and zoological gardens that would do credit to any country, and the grand plaza which is five hundred feet square. In the center is a floral garden, and a grand bronze fountain. The Cathedral stands on the east side, the most imposing structure in Peru.

Report says there are six thousand priests in Lima, but I have not counted them. There is but one Protestant minister, a clergyman of the Church of England, who has a small following of English residents, and conducts services in a private house. From the great number of churches we see in these cities we might conclude that our cousins are decidedly religious. The women, however, are the principal worshipers in church. There are no seats here in churches to seat a congregation. Each woman "going to meeting" carries with her a rug, which she spreads on the floor of solid bricks or cement, and kneels on it. Go into any of these churches at the hour for "mass," and you will see the body of the church more than half full of women, all kneeling on their mats, erect as statues, without any support for their bodies, except their knees, each one holding a little prayer-book in her left hand, while, at every jingle of the little bell at the altar, she crosses her forehead, breast, and face, and kisses her hand for its cunning in the ceremony. There is not a bonnet among them. Each one wears a black shawl of silk or French merino. One corner is drawn closely round the neck, making a close fit to the shoulders, with a hood for the head, leaving the face exposed, and the whole extending down to the knees. They look to " be all in mourning," and yet you are struck with the uniformity and neatness of their appearance.

Dr. Adam Clarke speaks of a bit of hard experience he suffered once at a prayer-meeting, where he kneeled down with no support but his two knees, and he said, "The unmerciful man prayed forty minutes." The Doctor believed in penitence, but not in penance. But these female cousins of ours remain from one to two solid hours, erect on their knees, displaying the patience of Job. The few men who attend, usually stand about the door, and some along the side walls. A few are sometimes found on their knees for a few minutes, but they can't stand it, and get up—a pity that their consciences are not as tender as their knees.

On Christmas-eve we attend an anniversary midnight mass to commemorate the birth of the illustrious Babe of Bethlehem in a stable. The night is far spent, the great audience-room is packed almost to suffocation; the priests are at the altar, mid the blaze of consecrated candles, surrounded by pictures and statues of dead saints, and of the Virgin Mother and her Son. Now an organ in the front gallery peals out a few notes and rolls

off a tune, accompanied by a solo in a mas-
culine voice of some feminine cousin of ours.
Now silence reigns, except the priestly mutter-
ings at the altar. Suddenly there is a tremendous breaking loose in the gallery, an awful
confusion of sounds—cymbals, tin-pans, horns,
lowing, cackling—a barnyard scene imitated,
a surprise at midnight among the men and
fowls of a stable, it beggars description. It
suddenly ceases, and after a season of silence
the organ and a solo singer take their turn;
then a repetition of the awful confusion of
sounds. These go on alternately for more than
an hour. Some of the performers in the stable
scenes behave irreverently, and the priest at
the altar rebukes them sharply, and troops
of them suddenly rush down the gallery
stairs like so many horses, and leave the
premises. I hardly knew whether that was
incidental, or the closing scene of the comedy.

All the while the women remain erect on
their knees looking at a book in their left,
and crossing themselves with their right hands
at every signal from the bell-boy at the altar.
In front of us stands an old man holding a
little girl by the hand. He looks around
about him, and up to the gallery, and seems

to take note of everything that is going on, but, alternately with his general observations, he utters his "Ave Marias" in weeping tones; I cannot be quite certain whether there was a flow of tears or not, but he meant well. He is evidently calling to remembrance his evil deeds and misspent hours which have so contributed to swell the records of the year just passing out.   Poor old coz.

The Foreigners' Church of Callao is a substantial building, containing an audience-room, 40 by 60 feet, a vestry, and two school-rooms. About seventeen years ago, William Wheelwright, the founder of the P. S. N. Co., passing through Callao on his way to New York, heard Rev. J. A. Swaney, an agent of the American Seamen's Friend Society, preach to his edification, in an inferior "hired house," and proposed that if Rev. Swaney would furnish him a plan and specifications of a church edifice suitable for Callao, he would, on his own account, have it framed in New York, and send it out.   Mr. Swaney accordingly got his friend Mr. DeCoursey to furnish the design and specifications, and in due time the frame was duly received.   The friends in Callao, however, having bought a lot, built a larger and more substantial edifice than the one contemplated, and worked all the materials of Mr. Wheelwright's gift into it. The property is deeded to the British, and American Consuls, and the manager of the P. S. N. Co., in trust for the foreign population of Callao. The management is intrusted to six gentlemen, elected annually by a majority of the subscribers and pew-holders. Unfortunately for the cause in Callao, before the house was completed, Mr. Swaney returned to the United States. He is an able minister of the Gospel, a prudent, good man, and had he held on in Callao, as Rev. Dr. Trumbull has done in Valparaiso, he might have done the great preparatory work for Peru, that the other man of God has done for Chile. For about fifteen years the Callao church has been under the pastoral care of different clergymen of the Church of England; but on our arrival, it was vacant, and had been closed for six weeks. For many years a sharp contention has been kept up between the "church party" and the "non-conformists." At the annual election last June, a non-conformist committee was elected, and they opened negotiations with Dr. Swaney to become their pastor, but owing to various unforeseen causes of delay, the question

5

has been in suspense ever since. Meantime, Dr. Swaney by letter informed the committee, one mail in advance, of my contemplated visit, so they received us gladly, and I served them during a period of two months. In that time I hunted up eighty-five English-speaking Protestant families, and made a pastoral list, and tried to pour oil on the troubled waters. Under very great discouragements we secured an increase in numbers, and interest in the congregations, and some good was done. The committee elected Bro. T——, who is an able minister of the Gospel, to be their pastor *pro tem*. The previous negotiations with Dr. Swaney still pending, we would not interfere with them, except to see that the pulpit should not be left without a minister.

The Pope's Nuncio arrived a few days after I commencd work in Callao, and promulgated an order, published in the Spanish papers, to close the Callao Protestant Church. We paid no attention to the order, nor did the local authorities, so the church was not closed, but the Nuncio soon found that his own position was not quite secure, for though he was received by the Peruvian Government, the "diplomatic corps" of other nations at the capital refused to recognize him. The point they made was, that since the Pope had lost his temporal power, he was not a sovereign, nor head of any nation, and therefore had no right of representation in the councils of any civil government.

Eight thousand persons have been buried in the foreigners' cemetery during the last twelve years—Protestants, principally English and German. What a body of buried agency that should have been utilized for God in "spreading scriptural holiness" through these lands!

Five bulls are killed in Callao every Sunday, specially in the interest of some church, or public charity. Each bull-bait is placarded on large wall-papers, with highly-colored pictures of bulls and lions engaged in mortal combat. Shooting, boat-racing, cock-fighting, and miscellaneous pleasure-taking, make up, for the most part, the exercises of the Lord's day in this country. Unfortunately the foreigners, who should truly represent the great Christian nations to which they belong, are too apt to slide down into these barbarous customs; but they have been as sheep without a shepherd.

I will tell you before we leave Callao how Satan put it into the heart of one of his servants to shoot me, and put a stop to the further extension of my self-supporting missions. Bro. T—— is a practical and scientific geologist, and for our needful exercise we often strolled on the south beach, gathering rare geological specimens of volcanic rocks.

On the morning of December 17, 1877, as we sat by the sea-shore, we saw about half a mile east of us a trooper dash up to the bluff, followed by armed foot-soldiers. They came by, two and two, about every hundred yards, evidently intending to cover the whole line of coast back to the city.

As we sat watching their movements, not suspecting personal peril, two soldiers with their breech-loading rifles came to the bluff opposite, and distant from us about forty yards. They halted and stood looking at us. In a few moments, two more came to view west of us, and distant about seventy-five yards. As soon as they caught sight of us, one of them, an intoxicated Indian, cocked his rifle, and in a half-bent position, with his gun elevated ready for an aim, he ran down the ridge of rubble stones toward us, till he reached more level standing-ground, and then stopped and took aim at us. We sprang to our feet, and held up our hands to show him that we had nothing, and were unarmed. He then ran about ten steps toward us, and took aim from his knee. Not satisfied with that chance for a sure shot, he ran about ten steps nearer, and aimed at us again, and then about ten steps still nearer, bringing the savage within thirty steps of us. There, with a rest from his knee, and as deliberate an aim as a soldier maddened with rum can take, he leveled his rifle at us. His fellow, and the two soldiers opposite, stood looking to see him shoot one or both of us. I saw from their attitude that if we should attempt either to run, or to resist, the whole quaternion of them would fire at us. This was all the work of a minute. I could not get my nerves shaken with fear in so short a time, but I thought fast. I did not believe that God would deliver either of us to the "bloody and deceitful men," but I had to do something, so I advanced rapidly on the Indian aiming at us. I curved a little to the left to avoid his direct range, and crossed with quick steps to the right, passing the muzzle of his gun but a few feet distant,

to give me vantage-ground for seizing him.
When nearly within arm's length he sprang to
his feet, and I grasped the barrel of his rifle.
My impulse was to wrest it from his hands
and throw it into the sea, and lay him level
with the ground, and I knew I had the power
to do it; but I felt certain in such a defense of
myself the other savages would fire on me; so,
as quietly as possible, I simply controlled his
gun, so that he could not shoot either of us.
Meantime I said, " Amigos, amigos,"—Friends,
friends. He then trailed his gun in his left
hand, and shook hands with me, but immediately drew up his gun to get a pull at Bro.
T——, who had followed close after me; but I
again seized the barrel of his rifle, and would
not allow him to get an aim, saying to him,
"Este mi hermano; este mi hermano,"—That
is my brother; that is my brother. He then
sprang back and tried to get another aim at
me, but I closed upon him, and held his gun
firmly, saying, "Americanos amigos, Americanos amigos,"—American friends, American
friends.

He seemed intent on killing, at least, one of
us, especially as the others were looking to see
him do it; but now he was cornered, and shook

hands with us both. Then he let down the hammer of his rifle, and began to jabber to us in a lingo that we understood not, when one of the soldiers on the bluff, who had watched the whole transaction, called him, and they all marched off together. We sat down and waited till the coast was all clear, and returned to our quarters. We learned afterward that they were in pursuit of thieves. To excite their valor, as in a revolutionary expedition, they must needs get furiously drunk; and not finding any thieves, the next thing was to kill an honest man or two. If they could have got an excuse, by our resistance or attempt at flight, for firing on us, they would have had a great story to tell of how they routed and dispatched the thieves. No thanks to them that life and reputation had not both been sacrificed together. No coroners in Peru. It is enough to know there that a man is dead. If I had my way with them, I would have them all converted to God. They need it.

But we must not leave Callao yet, as though we were frightened by an unseemly use of breech-loading rifles.

I had the pleasure of seeing Rev. Padré Vaughn here. He belongs to a high-class

English family of wealth, but is a humble, hard-
working man of God. He has devoted many
years to traveling and useful labors among all
the various nations of South America. Some
years since he collected funds there, for the
purpose of printing Bibles and Testaments in
the Spanish language, for circulation among the
peoples of South America. The Testaments
have been issued by Samuel Bagster & Co.,
and, under the sanction of the Pope, and many
bishops of the Roman Catholic church, are for
sale to the natives in nearly all the cities of
this continent. Five thousand copies of them
have been brought to Callao since my arrival.
The great miraculous events recorded are illustrated by wood-cuts. They are sold at a very
cheap rate, and are being circulated freely.
We have a Brother and Sister Peterson in Callao, humble servants of God, who are doing
much to spread the Word of God, and to bear
witness for Jesus.

Since my return to New York, I have received a letter from Bro. T——, whom I left
there to hold the fort, in which he says : "When
will Christianity in its purity dawn on these
lands ? A person cannot help liking the natives
of this country, notwithstanding their faults and

vices. In the name of humanity, what advantages have they had? But they will be reached by the Gospel, and embrace a true faith. Padré Vaughn has done a good work. They read his Testaments with deep interest. The demand is greater than the supply. I have given all mine away. The natives really are more accessible than the foreigners. Mrs. Peterson is a missionary among the natives. She visits the nunneries and hospitals, and tells them all of the saving power of Jesus. She went to hear the bishop last Sunday, and had a long talk with him on experimental religion. He told her that he would get Padré Vaughn to supply her with all the Testaments she could distribute. A brighter day is dawning for the Roman Catholics of South America." The bishop referred to is a Roman Catholic; Padré Vaughn, a priest of that church; Mrs. P——, a Scandinavian Lutheran, and the reporter a Methodist minister.

5*

V.

LEAVING Callao, January 3d, 1878, I embarked for Mollendo in the steamship *Aconcagua*. This floating palace, one of the P. S. N. Co.'s ships, which runs from Callao to Liverpool, is 431 feet long, 42 feet wide, with a registry of 4,106 tons. Her time from Callao to Valparaiso, 1,500 miles, is about ten days, stopping at many ports for freight, principally bar silver and copper. From Valparaiso to Liverpool, including stoppages, thirty-nine days.

We have among our passengers the wife and four little daughters of President Pardo, of Peru, going to join him in Chile. They are sociable and sensible. I made the acquaintance on this trip of a Peruvian cousin of ours, a fine specimen of a gentleman, a merchant from Arequipa, who kindly invited me to go home with him. He had been recently married to a Bolivian lady, and was on his way to meet her for the first time as his wife. It is lawful in this country to get married by proxy; so this gentleman, not having time to travel so far to participate in the ceremony, gave a gentleman friend authority to get married for him, and send the lady over the Andes to the man really meant.

On this little voyage I became acquainted with Mr. H. Parkman. He is a tall, square, noble-looking man, a Christian of the Presbyterian school, a conscientious, good man, and a teetotaler. He represents twelve Philadelphia hardware manufacturing establishments of twelve different varieties of hardware. They pay him two thousand dollars per month to open a market for their wares, which are of the latest and best improvements, and all of the best quality. He has a ton of specimens with him. He has spent some weeks in Lima, and received orders for fifteen thousand dollars' worth of his wares, cash to be paid into the bank on receipt of the invoices, which are forwarded to the banker. He only stops in the large cities; I stop at all the small ones as well. He gets high wages to put in the hardware—a good thing in its way. I pay my own expenses and work for nothing, for the love I have for my

dear cousins who sit in comparative darkness.
I want them to become acquainted with the
sinner's friend, my loving Saviour.

Bro. Parkman was asked one Sabbath in
Lima, by a merchant from the State of Maine,
to go with him to a bull-bait.

"I am astonished and horrified," replied
Parkman, "to find such a man as you, with
your superior Christian education, going to a
bull-fight on the Lord's day."

On another Sabbath a man asked him to accompany him to a masquerade ball. The man
from Maine spoke up and said, "It's no use
to ask Parkman to go to a ball. I asked him
last Sunday to go with me to a bull-fight, and
he gave me the biggest blowing up I ever got
in this country."

"Go to a masquerade ball," responded Parkman, "among a lot of licentious men and women, so corrupt that they are ashamed to let
their faces be recognized, and hence mask them.
I've got a wife and daughter in Philadelphia.
Suppose I should go with you to a masquerade
ball and get into collision with some ruffian and
get shot, and the news go home to my wife
and daughter! not to speak of my responsibility
to God."

I was glad to meet such a man as that from my country; the Lord bless him.

Mollendo is 300 miles south of Callao, irregularly built on hills and hollows, faced by precipitous bluffs, overlooking the rocks and breakers of the roadstead. It cannot lay claim to be a harbor, except a little cove, as a landing-place, formed by a small island to the south. It is a new place, without pavement or sidewalks, and just like a pioneer mining town in California. The mountains in the background are covered with green grass, a very unusual sight in Peru.

This is the western terminus of the "Mollendo, Arequipa and Puno" railroad, measuring from Mollendo to Puno a distance of 324 miles. The road to Arequipa, 107 miles, was built by Henry Meiggs in less than three years' time, at a cost of thirteen millions of silver dollars. The road thence to Puno, 217 miles, was built in less than four years, at a cost of twenty-seven millions of dollars. Henry Meiggs was contractor for this also, but sublet it to Mr. C——, who, 'tis said, cleared eight million dollars on the job. To give an idea of this stupendous work, the blasting on the two sections of the road through to Puno consumed three million pounds of powder; not a tunnel to dim the prospect on the whole line, and yet, by horseshoe curves and zigzag climbing, it ascends heavenward to the altitude of 14,660 feet. I have traveled over part of the road, and counted from one standpoint four ascending tracks on a single mountain face. Troy cars and New Jersey locomotives, it seems home-like.

Arequipa is the second city of Peru, with a population of 40,000, at an elevation of 7,560 feet above the Pacific Ocean. It is located near the base of Mount Misti, which rises to the height of 18,538 feet above sea level. Mount Misti is an active volcano. Its fires for many years were supposed to be extinct, but now from twenty-six apertures, down at the bottom of her great crater, emissions of steam observable are causing great apprehensions of peril among the 40,000 denizens below. The sudden flow of a river of burning lava, with a head of over 18,000 feet, would not give to the people of Arequipa half the chance of the people of Herculaneum and Pompeii to escape. Puno, with a population of 6,000, occupies an elevation of 12,547 feet above the sea, on the shore of Lake Titicaca, the fabled source of the Incas. Two steamers on this lake, which is 120 miles long, with an average width of twenty-five miles, connects part of the traffic of Bolivia with the Pacific Ocean at Mollendo.

A railroad from Juliaca, thirty miles this side of Puno, to Cusco, a distance of 259 miles, was contracted by Henry Meiggs, and sublet to my friend, Mr. T——, who has completed 86 miles of it, and is now proceeding with the work.

Among the wonders of this place is an aqueduct of eight-inch pipe tapping the Arequipa river, thirteen miles below the city, and extending through to Mollendo, a distance of ninety-four miles. It supplies all the stations on that stretch of line with water, and besides that, deposits daily into Mollendo 300,000 gallons of delicious water fresh from Andes snow.

This great work also was undertaken by Henry Meiggs for the sum of $3,000,000, and sublet to Messrs. J's and Thos. H—— at $2,800,000, and they cleared $800,000. Mr. Meiggs always received a high price for his work, but in return put in the best materials, and executed the work most substantially and elegantly.

The workshops of this great line are located at Mollendo, and employ a large number of English and American mechanics. The wages paid are as follows: Engineers, $250 per month; machinists, $150 on an average; firemen, natives, $90; conductors, $100; clerks from $100 to $150; treasurer, $250. My friend, Mr. S. B. Barnes, superintendent of motive-power both in the shops and on the road, receives $450 per month. These were the prices in paper currency when it was at par in the market. The currency has depreciated more than one-third from par value, but the wages have not been increased, nor have the fares on the road. It may be readily seen that this little town, not only for its own sake, but as a strategic base, for self-supporting educational and evangelizing work in regions beyond, is a point of great importance.

I arrived in Mollendo, Saturday, January 5th. Mr. R——, the British Consul, received me very kindly, and I had my head-quarters with him at the house of my friend, Mr. S——, the P. S. N. Co.'s agent, who has recently buried his wife, leaving him and "little Pat," their youngest, in very lonely bereavement. In company with Mr. B——, I visited most of the people Saturday night, and preached to a small but very attentive congregation on Sabbath. On Monday, A. M., assisted by my friend M. B——, I made up a subscription for passage and guarantee of support for a man of God from the United States.

I had brought some little blank books with me from New York. In one of these I wrote the following simple proposal: "Believing a school teacher, and a Gospel minister to be greatly needed in Mollendo, I propose to send hither a competent man, combining in himself the two-fold character of teacher and preacher. The first engagement to cover a period of at least three years. I respectfully ask the friends of this movement to contribute the funds for passage and a guarantee for support till the school shall become self-supporting. It will require $330 paper currency for passage, and at least $150 per month for sustentation.

"Respectfully submitted,

"WM. TAYLOR.

"MOLLENDO, June 7, 1877.

"We, the undersigned, concur in Mr. Taylor's proposal, and agree to pay the sums we here subscribe, for the purposes named, and do all else we can to make the undertaking a success." Then followed the double list of subscribers.

My first call was on an American railroad contractor.

Said he: "I am a Roman Catholic, and don't wish to put down my name, but I will give $50 (soles) to bring the man out, and $100 (soles) if you require it, and $30 (soles) per month for his support." (A sole is a Peruvian paper dollar as good as gold a few years ago, but now worth about seventy cents.) That was my first financial strike in South America. I next went to another extensive contractor, a Scotchman, in whose family I enjoyed a generous hospitality.

He said: "I'll guarantee $150 per month to support a man of the right sort, myself."

"I am greatly obliged by your kind offer, but I want to interest all the people of the town in him; and the only way to do that from the start is to let them take stock in him. The principle may be illustrated by a little chimney-sweep running down street in New York in the midst of a furious snowstorm. Some one shouted, 'Ho, Jack! which way are you going?' 'I, going to the missionary meeting. I've got a share in the concern. I gave a shilling last Sunday.' So we want every person available in this town to have a share in this concern."

We then called on shopkeepers, railway men, and others, who subscribed the passage-money required, also the monthly stipend, leaving my liberal friend but $28 instead of $150 per month to pay. I wrote in the little book my thankful acceptance of their liberality, and the closing of the agreement, naming three gentlemen as a committee and school-board to collect the funds and make all necessary arrangements for carrying our plans into effect.

VI.

ARICA AND TACNA.

On the 8th of January we sweep through the roaring serf at Mollendo, and embark on the steamship *Ayacucho*, 2,200 tons register, and in fifteen hours we cast anchor in the roadstead of Arica, 560 miles south of Callao. I present my papers to Geo. H. Nugent Esq., British and American Consul, a tall, commanding, fine-looking man. He receives me very kindly, but sees no hope of employing either school-teacher or preacher in Arica, and thinks it impossible for me to do anything in Tacna. The thought strikes me, "I had better not waste time here, but return to the steamer and proceed to Iquique, the next point on my list of places to be visited;" but having heard in Callao that the merchants of Tacna were an enterprising, noble class of men, I could not consent to pass them without an effort to do them good.

No train to Tacna till 3 P.M., and with several intervening hours on my hands, I must do something; so under the burning heat of a tropical sun, the hot sand almost crisping my shoe-leather, I climbed a mountain overlooking the sea. Its summit brings me within the sweep of the southwest trade winds that blow daily along this coast. How refreshing to the wayworn traveler! Here we get a grand view of the distant. Andes heights, and the intervening desert wastes. Beneath our feet is the town of Arica, containing a population of about 3,000 souls. We count five main streets at right angles from the shore, intersected by about the same number. About three miles north we see on an arid plain the United States war-steamer the *Wateree*. For a wonder in this desert land, we see on the north border of the town a few acres of garden land covered with vegetable products, and a variety of tropical fruit-trees. The percolating waters of an invisible river, seeking an underground passage from the mountains to the sea, are tapped by means of wells, and utilized by the gardeners.

The houses and courts are, as usual in this country, of the Oriental style, built of adobes, sun-dried brick, the most of them but one story in height. Among the exceptions to this class of buildings is a large two-story mansion of Mr. Alexander McLean, built of dressed stone. Mr. McLean is a Scotch gentleman, who has resided here over forty years; his wife is a fine specimen of a native lady, of a rugged, hardy type, who, though an old grandmother, wears the fresh appearance and manifests the vigor of a young woman in Scotland. These are the honored heads of a large respectable family connection residing in this region of country.

The principal church edifice of the town is an iron structure from New York. Some years age the President of Peru, His Excellency Don Balta, dispatched a special messenger to the United States with an appropriation of $200,000 to be invested in the construction of a church of the best style of Gothic architecture, to be shipped and put up at Ancon, a fashionable watering-place north of Lima.

Poor President Balta did not live to see his beautiful American church. His Minister of War, and two of his brothers who were colonels in the army, had been taken up by Señor Balta from a low station in life, and thus promoted to honor. They proved themselves to have been frozen snakes warmed into life in the bosom of their benefactor.

They concocted a revolution, which broke out in July, 1871. The said Minister of War assassinated the President as he sat unarmed in the executive mansion. He then by his rebel troops seized the garrison, dispersed the Senate and Congress then in session, and put a heavy cannon in position to pour a deadly volley upon the city. One of his officers, shocked at the thought of the promiscuous slaughter of unoffending men, women, and children, dared to remonstrate against the order. Instantly the arch rebel shot him, and in the next moment received a fatal shot himself from an unknown aim. The murdered and the murderer fell dead almost in the same second of time.

It was supposed that the sudden retribution was occasioned by a stray shot from without, but a man who witnessed the tragedy told me that one of his own soldiers shot him. The rebellion was extinguished during the night of the day in which it broke out. The next day the dead bodies of the three rebel brothers were exposed in the streets to the scorn of the populace, and then were burned.

President Balta's fine church had not yet arrived. The ship containing it, like the Peruvian ship of state, suffered a reverse, and had to return to New York, and at great cost transfer the church to another vessel. In consequence of the President's untimely death, the church was not taken to Ancon, but was landed at Callao, and thence by means of steamers brought in detached parts and finally erected here in Arica. As it now stands, it cost the Government, as I am informed by a resident who knows the whole history of it, half a million of dollars. The cost of such an edifice in New York would be about fifty thousand. I attended mass in it one Sabbath morning. In the midst of surrounding darkness, there on my knees, I had sweet communion with Him who is the light of the world. About sixty of our female cousins maintained their erect kneeling posture for more than an hour, while a few men stood round gazing at the performance. A dear feminine cousin near me sighed deeply, and to relieve her weak knees, occasionally sat on the floor, but resumed her kneeling posture at each ringing of the little bell at the altar, and repeated the ceremony of " crossing." I repeated the twenty-second Psalm, and got through with my prayers in less than half the time, and got a comfortable seat, and waited till the service closed.

It is said that one night Mr. Wesley chanced to bed with a fellow clergyman. Wesley spent a short time in prayer, retired, and in a few minutes was sound asleep. His companion spent an hour in reading his lessons and prayers, and then roused Wesley from his slumbers, and administered to him a reproof, saying: "What presumption in a man like you to make such a show of piety in the world as you do! You came in here, and got into bed in five minutes and went to sleep, while I have been engaged in my devotions for an hour."

Wesley replied, with a smile, "You get so far behind with your prayers, it takes an hour every night to make up lost time, but I keep prayed up." I find it a good thing to "keep prayed up," or as St. Paul puts it, to "pray without ceasing;" such live in the spirit of prayer, and abide in momently union with Jesus, as the branch in the vine, and they are the persons who most delight to "enter into their closet and pray to their Father," and participate in the sacred services of the sanctuary. For many years I have been in the habit occasion-

6

ally of going into the assemblies of our Roman Catholic brethren and sisters, to kneel down with them to pray for them and for myself, and if they had the freedom of the Jewish synagogue, where "the Scriptures were read every Sabbath day," and should say to me, "If you have any word of exhortation, brother, say on," I should be glad to tell them that the personal, living Lord Jesus had, according to the purpose of His coming, saved me from my sins.

As I am not allowed to do that, I can only pray for them, and on all suitable occasions show them the sympathy and love the Saviour hath put into my heart for all the families of the earth. Why should not the warm sympathy and love of every saved one go with the Saviour's blessing into every household in the world, for "in Him shall all the families of the earth be blessed"? Universal kindness to all men does not necessarily mean concurrence with the wrong theories or practices of any man. The God-man sat down and ate with publicans and sinners, and did not insult them by any obtrusive, untimely attack upon their errors and wickedness, and yet he did not compromise the truth, nor endorse their errors, but by his winning ways and wisdom he induced them to open the doors of their hearts, and light from heaven entered, and thus they saw their errors and their sins, and felt a heaven-wrought desire to be led to a better life.

Arica is a place greatly distinguished for its sublime earthquakes and tidal waves. From Mr. Squier's able work on the Incas, published by Harper Brothers, I copy the following description of the earthquake of 1868, written by an officer of the U. S. gunboat *Wateree:*

"At about twenty minutes past five o'clock we saw immense clouds of dust some ten miles south of Arica, which came nearer and nearer. Then we saw the peaks of the mountains begin to wave to and fro like reeds in a storm. As the wave approached us we saw great rocks rent from the mountain heights, and with large mounds of earth they rolled down their sides. Very soon the whole earth was shaking. When the convulsion reached the mole, it also began to move, and the town commenced to crumble into ruins. The noise was like the rumbling echoes of thunder, the explosive sounds like those of the firing of a heavy battery, terrific and deafening. The whole soil of the country, as far as we could see, was

moving first like a wave in the direction from
south to north; then it trembled, and at last
it shook heavily, throwing into heaps of ruins
two-thirds of all the houses of Arica. Shock
after shock followed. In several places sul-
phurous vapor issued from openings in the
earth. At this juncture a crowd of people
flocked to the mole, seeking boats to take
refuge on the vessels in the harbor. As yet
the shipping felt not the least commotion from
the disturbances on the land. After the first
shock there was a rest. The *Wateree* and the
Fredonia sent their surgeons ashore to assist
the wounded. Between fifty and sixty people
of the town had reached the mole by this time
to take the boats. But the surgeons had hardly landed, and but few others had entered the
boats, when the sea quietly receded from the
shore, leaving the boats hard aground. When
the water had reached the depth of extremely
low tide, then all at once, on the whole levee
of the harbor, it commenced to rise. It appeared at first as if the ground of the shore
was sinking. The mole was carried away, and
the people on it were seen floating. The water
rose to the height of thirty-four feet above
high-water mark, and overflowed the town,

ARICA AND TACNA.   125

sweeping down what the earthquake had left. All this work of the waters was done in five minutes. Then the water rushed back into the ocean more suddenly than it advanced upon the land. This awful spectacle of destruction by the receding flood had hardly been realized when the sea rose again, and now the vessels in port began dragging their anchors. The water rose to the same height as before, and on rushing back, it brought not only the débris of a ruined city with it, but even a locomotive and tender, and a train of four cars were seen carried away by the force of the waters. During the advance of the sea inland, another terrific shock, lasting about eight minutes, was felt. At this time all around the city the dust formed in clouds, obscuring the sky, and rendering the land quite invisible. Then was heard the thundering approach of a sea wave, then was seen a sea wall of perpendicular height, to the extent of from forty-two to forty-five feet, capped with a fringe of bright glistening foam, sweeping over the land, stranding far inland the United States war-steamer *Wateree*, the Peruvian frigate *America*, and an English merchant ship and many others."

Mr. Nugent and family and many others

fled to the hills after the first shock, before the tidal wave came. He told me that he was induced thus to flee to the mountains from having read an account of the earthquakes in the West Indies the preceding year, and that there the tidal wave immediately followed the earthquake shocks. Thus he had the advantage of the wretched people who did not read the papers, and who, in their ignorance, rushed for the boats to seek a refuge on the ships. The *Wateree* was a God-send to the destitute thousands who had lost all but life. She had all her stores in perfect order; having been built for river service during the war, and drawing but six feet of water, she was carried on the crest of the waves a quarter of a mile inland, and set down on a level plain. Not a man was lost, except one poor fellow who was in the boat when the ship was carried ashore. The captain generously supplied the sufferers with blankets, provisions, and whatever the ship contained that they needed. I have heard many of them speak gratefully of the relief they got from the *Wateree*. The tidal wave of last May lifted the *Wateree* from her bed and carried her about two miles north, broke her back, and set her down much nearer to the sea, where she now appears to be "a vessel of wrath, fitted only for destruction." Thus it seems that the tidal wave of last May was as high, or higher, than the one of 1868, which sent this noble ship ashore. We walk over many acres of desolation in Arica. Railway works, workshops, foundry, freight and engine-houses, stores and dwellings of the town, caught up from their foundations, skaken to fragments, and scattered to the winds. There are heaps of rail-cars upturned; here, a steam-ship in pieces, engine there, boiler yonder. There lies a great iron turning-lathe thrown from some wreck, and a war-ship's supply of cannon balls, all discharged at one shot, lie in a pile of unnumbered tons; further on a lot of mill-stones; and there are twenty-four beautiful truncated iron columns, ship-loads of iron in all shapes, to tell of blasted hopes and of fortunes lost in Arica.

At 3 P.M. on the 9th of January, I took the rail for Tacna, thirty-nine miles distant, at an elevation of 2,000 feet above sea-level. A hot, dusty travel over a desert, till we see in the distance the green gardens and orchards of Tacna.

It is a town of about 14,000 inhabitants.

Living streams, fresh from the Andes, flow through some of the principal streets, and water the neighboring vineyards and gardens; It is an oasis in the desert.

We arrived at 6 P.M. I had a letter of introduction from our Consul at Arica to Mr. A——, of Tacna, so I engaged a boy to carry my portmanteau and conduct me to his house. We had gone but a few rods, when my porter employed a smaller boy to do the carrying business, while he, as the original contractor, should play the gentleman, and get a fee for himself and another for the little Cholo who carried the load. Coming to a hotel, I left my luggage, and went beyond the town, and found the man I sought. I gave him the letter, and explained to him the object of my mission. He was kind, but quite unbelieving. He was quite sure that I could do nothing in Tacna, so I left him, and returned to the hotel. At the supper-table I made the acquaintance of a young English gentleman, and tried to find out how many English-speaking families resided in the town, and what the prospect for educational work. He could give me no encouragement. Later in the evening, I strolled down town to the plaza, where many gentle-

men and ladies were promenading, and others
reposing on the public seats prepared and
waiting for the weary; so I sat down on one
beside a German, who informed me that there
were a few English and many German families
in Tacna, and he believed that a good English
school was one of the great needs of the city.
I was glad I met with that German; he did me
good.

I returned, and retired to bed at 9 P.M.,
but not to sleep. It was one of those nights
of waking visions such as I used to have in
Bombay, when God made known His way to
his poor ignorant servant. I don't mean miraculous visions, but an intelligible manifestation
of God's will, showing me my path of duty
through unexplored regions where there were
no sign-boards nor blazed trees to indicate
the right way. The revealings of that night
widened my field of operations, narrowed my
work, and shortened my stay for the present
in South America, so as to put me back to
New York early in May of this year. My
way was widened so as to send good school-
teachers where preachers would not be received
at all; my work narrowed, so that instead of
staying to plant churches, as I did in India, I

6*

was first to send men to lay the foundations; then, after a term of years, return to build; time shortened by extending my preparatory work rapidly along the coast, and hasten home to find and send the workers.

Tacna was to be my first departure from the old line of purely evangelistic work, to the new line of school-work simply, where nothing more is at present possible. I had it all mapped out before morning, and hence the first thing was to write my proposal for the merchants of Tacna to found an English school. I had it clearly stated, so that they could see the object, and the way to attain it, at a glance, and have nothing to do but subscribe the funds and sign the papers. I went into the coffee-room and sat down by a young man who I thought might understand the English language. I found him to be an intelligent gentleman of French extraction, but a native of Minnesota. He was my providential man for the moment.

I laid my case before him, and he said:

"I don't think you can do anything in Tacna, but the man whom you should see is Mr. Wm. Hellman. If you can get him to see as you do, you'll succeed. He'll not come to his office till 11 A.M.; but I am just now going down town, and will show you his place of business."

At the hour designated, I presented myself to Mr. Hellman, and stated my object, and showed him my written proposals.

He replied: "It is a thing very much needed here; but this whole country is badly demoralized, and I fear that nothing can be done."

"Well, my dear sir, you are hardly prepared to turn them all over to the 'old scratch,' without at least one more effort for the education of the rising generation. If you can succeed in giving a good education and a good moral training to one boy of thousands who are running wild around here, he may be the coming man of mark to raise this country to a higher level. What I propose, too, is not like a great railroad venture, involving a hazardous outlay of funds, but a very economical enterprise, with promise of large returns for the good of the country."

"I have brought out governesses at different times from England, but they get discouraged, and do but little good."

"Now, last of all, you had better try one live

American to help you found a good English school in Tacna."

" But, I am not the man to lead in such a movement; you should go to Mr. Outram."

" Very well; if Mr. Outram leads, will you follow ? "

" Yes, I will do my part."

" Shall I go alone, to wait on Mr. Outram, or will you go with me ? "

By this time he had put on his hat, and said, " Come, let us go."

Just outside he met the banker, Señor Don Basadre, and began to explain the project to him. I said, " Fetch him along." So on they came, and I was introduced to Mr. Outram, a merchant prince. My friend, Mr. H——, saved me the trouble of telling my story, by stating the case himself, and advocating it eloquently.

In a few moments Mr. Jones came in, and Mr. H—— said to him: " Mr. Jones, you remember we were talking the other day about the great need of an English school in this town, and were devising how it could be brought about. Now here is a benevolent gentleman, who has come to help us in this very thing."

Mr. O—— said: "How long can you re-main with us?"

"I expect to return to Arica to-morrow morning."

"This is our mail-day for Bolivia, and we are all extremely busy, but we think well of your proposition, and I think we will write you a favorable response to Valparaiso, if that will do."

"Thank you, sir, that will do, if you cannot do better; but this is a very plain case, which need not consume much of your time, and my success here will help to open my way along the coast."

He made no reply, but took up his pen and signed the articles of agreement.

Then Mr. Jones signed. Meantime Mr. H—— made some allusion to California, and said that he lived in San Francisco in 1853.

"Do you remember a man called Father Taylor, who preached every Sabbath after-noon on the plaza to the masses?"

"Yes, I remember Father Taylor very well."

"That same Father Taylor has come now to help you here in Tacna." We both rose up and shook hands as old friends. So we proceeded and completed our preparatory business in about half an hour more. I asked for a subscription of £30 sterling to pay passage of a single man from New York to Tacna, and the guarantee of $100 per month for his support till the school could be made self-supporting to the extent of at least that amount. Eight generous gentlemen signed the papers, obliging themselves voluntarily to give £90 sterling for passage, and $200 per month guarantee for a male and female teacher, a good man and his wife—our engagement to cover a period of at least three years.

Tacna carries on a large trade, principally of wool and copper, with Bolivia, transported across the near range of the Andes on the backs of llamas and mules. The llama carries a burden of one hundred pounds, the mule three hundred pounds. Arica is the port of entry, and its lists of imports and exports will convey an idea of the strength of this current of commerce.

Her imports consist of cottons, woolens, linens, silks, furniture, hardware, earthenware and glassware, oilman's stores, wines, malt liquors and spirits, and medicines.

The sources and value of these imports for
1876 are as follows, in silver coin:

Chile, ...	$116,652 48
France, ...	545,995 99
Germany, ...	455,325 35
Great Britain, ...	686,800 77
United States, ...	116,652 48
Total, ...	$1,854,171 08

The exports of Arica consist principally of
Peruvian bark, copper ore, tin ore, bar tin and
bullion, sheep's wool, alpaca, llama and vicuña
wool, coffee, tobacco, brandy, hides and skins
in great variety, etc. Total value in silver
dollars for 1876, amounts to the sum of
$4,816,686.09; more than one-half of this
amount was in gold and silver bullion and
coin. I am indebted to the kindness of our
Consul for these facts. He lost $50,000—his
all, except a town lot—by the earthquake of
1868. Having a large family to support and to
educate, now numbering twelve robust, healthy
children, he determined to dig a hole in the
ground, on his own town lot, and "make by
fresh water what he had lost by salt." He happily struck the "invisible river," which sent
forth copious supplies of clear pure water

already filtered by its percolation through the rubble and sand. He got up a water company, with capital to the amount of $200,000. They employ two steamers to carry water one hundred and eight miles south to Iquique, and to other dry ports still more remote. Prior to this, Iquique had to depend on distillation of fresh water from salt, which was sold at eight cents per gallon. Arica delivers it to the Iquique people for two cents per gallon.

The water-tank at Iquique has an elevation of sixty-seven feet, and contains one thousand tons of water. Though Mr. N—— gets the water out of his own land, he has to pay the municipality a tax of $4,000 per year, and $964 port dues, to get it out, and pays Iquique $1,200 per year duty to get it in, and yet the business pays a good dividend. I had the promise of a passage in the water steamer, *Maria Louisa*, Captain Wm. Taylor, to Iquique, on Friday the 11th, and hence my haste to return from Tacna; but the said steamer did not get off till Monday P. M., so I had to pay $1 per night for poor lodgings, and wait patiently. I was, however, made welcome at the table of our consular friend and his kind family. The Lord bless them. The railway works of the

Arica and Tacna railroad, twice torn to pieces within nine years by tidal waves, have recently been removed to Tacna, two thousand feet above ordinary sea-level, where they hope to have no further annoyance from the sea.

P. S.—New York, June 5th, 1878. True to their engagement, my merchant princes of Tacna forwarded the passage funds, and I have appointed Professor Alexander P. Stowell, Mrs. Stowell, and a music-teacher besides, to found the school. They are to sail from New York for Tacna on the 30th of this month.

VII.

ON Monday, January the 14th, as the sun in grand reflected radiance was sinking beneath the horizon of the great waters of the West, we embark on Captain Taylor's steamer *Maria Louisa.*

She has a freight of 85,000 gallons of pure water from Arica wells, bound for Iquique, distant one hundred and eight miles. She has in tow the *San Carlos,* containing 200,000 gallons of water, bound for Pasagua, which is an important port for the saltpeter trade, a little over half-way to Iquique.

Captain Taylor is a very gentle, kind Scotchman, and son-in-law of Captain Wilson, British Vice-Consul of Callao. When I informed the captain of our contemplated school in Tacua, the tears seemed to fill his eyes.

138

"Ah, that touches me! I sent my wife and four children to Scotland, three years ago, for the children's education. Our oldest is but twelve years old now. To endure this wretched separation from one's family till they all get their education, is a long, lonesome lane to travel. I do hope you will succeed in founding a good school in Tacna. I will bring my wife and children back, and settle them there, and have my children educated where I can see them every week."

Within the last forty years, thousands of cases of this sort have transpired along the coast. Many hundreds of children have been educated in Valparaiso, but the board and tuition of a pupil there for one year costs about $800. A man with a large family and small means cannot stand that rate of expenditure. Others send their children to the United Kingdom and to Europe for their education. Some return and do well, but a very large number, freed from the wholesome checks of parental influence, not to speak of the molding power of the parent in the development of a child's character, fall into bad associations, and form habits which ruin them for life. I met a gentleman of fortune a few days ago, who spent a large sum of money on the education of his two sons in London. They returned to their kind, hopeful father last year. To the great grief of the father, he soon found that his elder son, instead of being a gentleman and a competent business-man as he hoped, was a confirmed drunkard, and died in *delirium tremens* before the year was out.

The younger proved to be a worthless spendthrift, unfit for any business. Many others send their wives and children home together, that the mother may superintend the education of the children. In some cases this works well, but in most cases disastrously, at least to the parents.

To found a good English school, therefore, in every English-speaking community on this coast, and that by a liberally educated Gospel minister, who can exercise a pastor's care over the people also, is the blessed work which God has sent me to initiate in this land.

Yet, blessed as that may be in itself, it is not the end of my mission to South America, but simply a means of blessing to the thirty-eight millions of the Latin races who are our kindred and near neighbors, from whom we should withhold no good thing.

Iquique is the principal port of the province of Tarapaca, the native province of General Castillo, the Abraham Lincoln of Peru; slavery expired at the edge of his sword; a great general in the field, a wise statesman, one of the best administrators that ever filled ·the presidential chair of that republic, and withal, a full-blooded Indian, one of the old Incas risen from the dead.

As we near our anchorage at Iquique on Tuesday morning, the 15th of January, Captain Taylor points to the wreck of a ship he lost there last year. This can hardly be called a harbor; it is a roadstead, protected on the south by a little island, on which a steamship lies high on the rocks. She was anchored there, quite unbroken, by the tidal wave of the 9th of last May.

Captain T—— introduced me to half a dozen leading gentlemen of Iquique, who gave me but little encouragement. All admitted the great need of a school, and some thought a preacher might do some good; but the thing had been tried in good times, and the result was utter failure, and now, in these hard times, it was all nonsense to attempt such a thing. I had met that objection at all preceding ports, and had become somewhat familiar with the facts, and with both sides of the argument.

A very good and able doctor of divinity from Liverpool visited this coast some years ago, to find out from personal observation its spiritual requirements, and devise means to meet them. He meant well, but did not adopt the right method. He did not commit the people here in any way, but committed himself by the promise of help from a generous people at home. His plan was defective, in that he was aiming to apply the missionary principle of dependence to a people who were as able to support school-teachers and Gospel ministers as the average of people who give missionary money at home. To treat such either as paupers or heathens is an insult : though they may appreciate the motive and receive the misdirected effort with thanks, the result is failure. A thing to live must embody a sound vital principle.

Later still a learned bishop traversed the coast from Panama to Patagonia. In some places he got large sums of money subscribed. In such places, and in others where he hoped that the people would raise the funds to support a clergyman, the bishop appointed "councils" to co-operate with him in carrying out his pious purpose. He "struck the lead," but his machinery was too unwieldy and too costly for this coast, and was entangled with too much tape for the times here. The supplies of men had to come through another bishop eight thousand miles away. Here in Iquique the good bishop got four thousand dollars subscribed, and the people really thought it meant business. After many months of suspense, the "council" received a letter from the great metropolitan master, stating that he had given due consideration to their case, and could only state, that unless the people of Iquique would pledge themselves to build a church, and guarantee a salary of $5,000 per year, he could not send them a clergyman. The people were neither able nor willing to assume such a responsibility.

The chaplain in Callao for a few years past received a salary of $4,000 in gold, and his perquisites, it is said, exceeded another thousand, for he made a charge for every baptism, and for reading the funeral service over a poor dead sailor he presented his bill for sixteen dollars to the Consul, who paid it. I don't pen these facts invidiously, but

to show how impossible it appears to the
people in smaller towns to have a preacher.
If I had the men at command at once, I
could station forty of them where they could
do a great educational and evangelical work,
and get a support, in no place less than
$100 per month; but I have to get a people
whose confidence has been broken down to subscribe funds to pay the passage and guarantee
the support of men yet to be selected and sent
out after a period of six months or more. It
requires great presumption, or great faith in
God and man, to undertake such a work. I
have great faith in God, and great faith in
man, and in the past both have exceeded my
expectations.

Nevertheless, coming as an unofficial stranger, my nationality, my church relations, and
the prospect of supplies of men from my country are urged as a serious ground of objection
to the undertaking, by some moneyed men
whose influence falls into the opposite scale;
my success will be a providential miracle, and
I will give all the glory to God. The great
risk at the start is the raising of the passage-
money. All admit that if a good man was on
the ground there would be no difficulty at all

about getting all the funds required for his support. The English-speaking people of this coast are very much like the pioneer Californians, they make and spend their money freely, and give liberally to any worthy object. I could collect the passage-money as I proceed, but it is too long to hold it. The opposition would laugh at the men giving it with an innuendo remark and shrug of the shoulder to the effect that the man they trusted had run away with their money. Hence, I would not handle a dime of their funds. The sweep of counter currents for six months imperils their confidence. The danger is that doubt may predominate, and prevent them from collecting and forwarding the funds; but I will trust and work, and win, by the mercy of God, and the surviving faith and liberality of the people.

Well, here we are in Iquique, the place we have read about, that "was swallowed up by an earthquake in 1868." It was not " swallowed up," but it was terribly shaken to pieces; the tidal wave swept over a large portion of it, and of its 13,000 people, it was supposed that one-half of them were drowned. The town suffered terribly also by the earthquake

7

of last May. The people fled to the hills and escaped the tidal wave, but the kerosene lamps left burning in their houses were upset by the violence of the shocks, and set the town on fire. There were three fire-companies in the town, two German and one English. They rushed out with their engines to quench the flames. The tidal wave saved them that trouble, but swept away the engines and hose of both the German companies, and the Eng- lish company made a very narrow escape.

Iquique has a population of about 12,000. Its principal export is nitrate of soda or salt- peter. It is brought from the coast range of mountains back of the town. The villages of Limeña and La Noria, thirty-four miles distant, are large sources of supply. I visited those diggings, and the rocks that cover hundreds of acres of those dry mountains are of pure white salt. The saltpeter is found in loads a few feet below the surface. Much of it is dug out in a pure crystallized form, but it is boiled, filtered, and dried, and then put into sacks containing about three bushels each. Those deposits are connected with Iquique by rail- way. The main track is seventy miles in length, with side tracks, making a total of about one hundred miles. This road was built by a native company, with borrowed English capital. The company could not meet their obligations, and the road and running stock were passed into the hands of the capitalists whose money built it, to be run by them till the whole debt, with interest, shall be paid. In their hands, it is a paying concern. The railroad works in Iquique constitute a very important part of the town.

The following brief exhibit will convey an idea of the commercial importance of this town and its chief industry. Forty ships were at anchor in its harbor when I was there. I boarded twenty-eight of them one morning before breakfast. I can't say that I breakfasted very early that day. Most of them were large, first-class iron ships. The number and nationality of the ships freighted here last year, 1876, were as follows:

English,	.	.	.	.	.	.	.	242
German,	.	.	.	.	.	.	.	58
French,	.	.	.	.	.	.	.	53
Norway,	.	.	.	.	.	.	.	8
North America,	.	.	.	.	.	.	17
Italy,	.	.	.	.	.	.	.	4
Belgium,	.	.	.	.	.	.	.	1
Holland,	.	.	.	.	.	.	.	1

Chile,	.	.	.	.	.	.	1
Russia,	.	.	.	.	.	.	1
Nicaragua,	.	.	.	.	.	.	2
Denmark,	.	.	.	.	.	.	1
	Total,	.	.	.	.	.	389

The aggregate quantity and value of the saltpeter thus exported in 1876, was 7,050,764 quintals, valued at thirteen shillings per quintal, a round sum of over twenty-two million of hard dollars ($22,033,637). The nationality of the ships will give an approximate, but not an entirely accurate idea of the markets of the world to which this product of Iquique has been shipped, and is being shipped continually.

Mr. Ralph Garratt, a kind-hearted Canadian gentleman, the station-master, secured for me, through the obliging disposition of Mr. Rowland, the manager, the free use of a well-furnished upper room in the company's large two-story building. Mr. Garratt also gave me a free welcome to his table. His family consists of a kind, gentle Peruvian wife, four children, an African nurse, a Chinese cook, and seven dogs. Mr. G——, with a religious education, had not heard preaching for sixteen years prior to my visit; not unwilling to hear, but how could he

"hear without a preacher"? He was anxious
for a school, and for preaching as well, and
offered to subscribe liberally at the first mention of my mission. I was advised to secure
the co-operation of John Nairn, Esq., a reliable
Presbyterian gentleman from Liverpool, who
has resided in this country ever since the year
1841. He is married to a native lady, and
has brought up his family on this coast.

Mr. N—— received me very kindly, and
was quite willing to assist in any way possible.
By his advice we got the British Vice-Consul
to issue a circular inviting the principal men
of the town to a meeting at the Consulate that
evening, Tuesday the 15th. We had a fair attendance, but not many of the "men of means."
I first submitted to them the proposal to send
out a man and his wife to found a male and
female school, the man to be pastor as well,
for the English-speaking people. The question
was discussed, and the conclusion was reached
that, however desirable, they could not, these
hard times, raise so much money as would be
required for so large a venture. I then submitted an alternate proposal, which I had
previously written, to send a single man who
should be qualified to teach and preach. They

cheerfully concurred in that, and appointed John Nairn, Esq., to accompany me to call on the people for subscriptions.

The simple proposition I had written in my little book, accepted by the meeting at the British Consulate, was as follows: " The city of Iquique being in need of an English school of high grade, for the education of the children of English, German, and the better class of Peruvian families in all the branches of a good English education, and the classics, and also of a good Gospel minister for the English-speaking population, travelers, and seamen in this port, I propose to send hither a competent man combining in himself the twofold character of school-teacher and pastor. Religious creeds not to be interfered with, nor taught in the school.

" I therefore respectfully ask gentlemen interested in this good enterprise, to subscribe the sum of £35, sterling, to pay his passage to Iquique, and a monthly subscription amounting to an aggregate of one hundred silver dollars per month for his support, until the school shall become self-supporting. Passage subscription to be paid by the middle of April of this year, the other monthly, after the arrival of the teacher. This agreement to cover a period of at least three years.

"Respectfully submitted,

"WM. TAYLOR.

"IQUIQUE, January 17, 1878.

"We the undersigned concur in Mr. Taylor's proposal, and agree to pay the sums we here subscribe, and do all else we can to make the undertaking a success.

"IQUIQUE, January 17, 1878."

This was followed by a record of fifty names, with subscriptions exceeding the amount required. The committee elected at a public meeting of the people were J. N. Satler, German Consul, treasurer; J. Martin, secretary; J. Nairn, Esq., collector for the city; Thomas Greenwood, collector in railway works and the harbor; Ralph Garratt to provide a place for religious services.

At our meeting at the British Consulate, Mr. Garratt was appointed to provide a preaching place for me during my sojourn in the town. He furnished the railway station with seats and lights, and I preached there on Wednesday and Thursday evenings of that week, and

at one and half-past seven P. M. the following
Sabbath. Our congregations did not exceed
forty persons, but were very attentive, and
there was some awakening of real religious interest, like the outside melting of an iceberg.
It required more time than I could command
to secure a thorough soul-converting work.

We had no public services after Sabbath, as
I expected to leave on Monday, by the coasting steamer *Ballistas*, Captain Perrot; but by
detention of the steamer I did not get a passage until the following Thursday. I had
some trying delays and discouragements in
Iquique, with many encouragements. I found
one young man in Iquique who appears to be
decidedly religious, Thomas Greenwood, from
London. He has been in this desert land
nearly four years. A Mr. Reader for a year
or two had held small meetings in a read-
ing-room in the railway company's works.
When he left some months ago, Mr. G——
took his place, and has kept up the meetings
of about half a dozen persons, but had become so discouraged that he sent his wife
home to London, and was arranging to give up
his place as a foreman in the railway workshops, worth 350 soles per month, and return

to London to work as a common mechanic for less than half that amount of pay, just to be with God's people; but when he saw what I was doing he was filled with joy, and took my book to the men in the shops and got subscriptions amounting to 100 soles per month. He at once wrote requesting his wife to return to Iquique, where he now expects to devote his life to business and to the work of God. I found a man in those shops who told me that he was four years a minister in the Wesleyan Conference, but got out during the excitement of "the Reform movement," and came to this coast in 1837. He has had a dreary time, but is feeling his way back to the "old paths, and the good way," with a sincere intention to "walk therein."

I found in Mr. J. M. Nicholls, head foreman in the railway works, a true friend of our enterprise.

The most striking incident of my visit to Iquique occurred on the evening of the 23d of January. Mr. G——, a young Englishman, who was somewhat awakened at my meetings, came at different times to talk, and get me to advise him what to do to be saved. His wife is a Chileno lady, and in getting married, as

7*

usual in such cases, the priest obliged him to
sign an obligation to be a Roman Catholic.
That being against his conscience, he had been
burdened with it during all the intervening
years, and was anxious to see his way out.
Well, on the evening of the 23d, he was in my
room; I talked to him about an hour and then
prayed with him. Just as I was closing my
prayer, while yet on my knees, the bottom
seemed to be going out generally. The foundations of the earth were shaken, and it appeared as though "the mountains might be
carried into the midst of the sea."

My man sprang to his feet, saying, "We
must get out of this."

"Never mind, I suppose it will be over
soon."

"No, if we don't get out at once the door
will be jammed, and then we can't get out."

With that he went and tried to open
the door. It was already jammed, but by
pulling and jerking he got it open, and went
out. I looked about the room, and got my
hat, and was going out of the door, when I
remembered what my friend had told me, half
an hour before, about the earthquake of last
May overturning the lamps and setting the

town on fire; so I returned and blew out my
candle. The motion meantime was that of
sudden jolting, like a wagon on a corduroy
road. When I got out into the veranda, I
had to go a distance of fifty feet to get to the
stairs leading down and out. I could hardly
keep on my feet. It was like walking the
deck of a ship in a chopping sea in the Bay
of Biscay. Descending the stairs I held on to
the railing, and thus kept up. My friend was
waiting for me below. By the time I got on
to the ground the violent shocks abated, followed by vibrations every few minutes. We
already saw lights on the hills, and others moving rapidly up. Every dog in town seemed
to expect the engulphing sweep of the tidal
wave, and with the people ran to the hills,
making the darkness hideous by their barking.

Mr. G—— said, "Excuse me, I must go
and look after my wife and children."

I then walked up to Mr. Garratt's. He
and his family, with the help of some of his
watchmen, were busily engaged providing bed-
ding, water and provisions for lodging on the
hills.

Said Mr. G——, "This is heavier than the
earthquake of last May, and the sea will be

upon us in a quarter of an hour, if we don't
get away to the hills. So I got my Bible and
a wrapper and went with them. It was very
dark, and, except the hideous barking of the
dogs, awfully quiet.

"Ah," said Mr. G——, "this dreadful still-
ness precedes the tidal wave. It will sweep
this town in ten minutes." It was awful to
think of forty ships grinding each other to
pieces, and be dashed and broken up amid the
ruins of the town. Never having had my
nerves shaken by such scenes before, I did
not feel half the alarm that the residents manifested, but I quietly prayed to God to spare
the town and the shipping. I thought of
Abraham pleading for Sodom, and begged the
Lord, if there were not ten righteous men in
the place, possibly there might be three, and
to spare it for their sake, and if not three,
then in mercy to give the place a chance to
benefit by the ministry of the man of God
to be sent to Iquique. We waited on the
hill about an hour, when Mr. G—— and I
walked back. He stopped at his house, and I
went to his office, and met a number of leading
gentlemen of the town. The earthquake had
stopped the clock in the railway office at three

minutes to 8 P.M., so we thus knew the exact time of the shocking event.

About 10 P.M. I went to my room and retired to bed. Happily the sea remained quiet, but all seemed to be painfully apprehensive of a recurrence, and perhaps the next time the earth might open her mouth and swallow the whole town.

I searched to see that I was wholly submitted to God, and quietly entrusted soul and body to the care of my Saviour. I could not call to mind one act of my life on which I could base any hope of heaven, but sweetly resting my all in the hands of Jesus, I had sweet assurance that all was well. As I was dropping off to sleep I counted ten shocks that caused a creaking of the timbers of the building, but I soon fell asleep, and waked up in the clear light of a peaceful morning.

P. S.—New York, June 5th, 1878. I will add that the secretary of our committee in Iquique, J. Martin, Esq., has duly forwarded the passage-money, and I have appointed Professor J. W. Collier, B.A., to that important station, and he is to sail from New York for Iquique on the 31st day of July, proximo.

VIII.

By the kind invitation of Captain Perrott, I took passage on his little coasting steamer, the *Balistas*, from Iquique, fifty-five miles, to the guano-loading port bearing the above hard name, pronounced Pahbelyone da Pecah. Our very small craft was loaded down to her lowest safe depth. The deck was piled up with lumber, pine boards from Oregon, and with baled hay. Mr. White, the kind-hearted Scotch engineer, offered me his bunk below for the night, but, with thanks for his kindness, I preferred the soft side of a pile of boards on the deck, where I could enjoy the breeze. My deck companions were three Cholo cousins of ours ; one, an old man, pretty drunk. He went to sleep on a bale of hay, and by a lurch in the night, was thrown headlong on boxes and boards piled up level with the top of the bulwarks ; six inches further he would have gone overboard. He cut his head badly, and lost his hat. Poor old coz !

No. 2 was a very rotund, well-conditioned-looking man, who could speak a few words of English. He was full of bad rum and nonsense. His capacious pockets contained each a bottle of "evil spirits," and in one of them a six-shooter. He seemed to have a musical turn of mind, and occasionally entertained us by blowing a child's musical instrument. He had with him his little son of about seven years. The dear little fellow was fearful for himself and for his father, and tried to keep him from going to sleep, often fretting, and begging his father to sit up. He seemed to dread what so nearly happened to the old man—a struggle in a drunken dream that might tumble him into the sea. Poor little fellow, with such a father, what will be his life-course and end? Cousin John Chinaman served us with good coffee—a genial, manly fellow was he.

Next morning, within a mile of our port, Mr. White pointed to a small lone dwelling on the rocky shore of a little bay, said: "Do you see that house?"

"Yes."

"That is all that remains of the town of Cheneviye. It contained a population of about 400, and the tidal wave of last May swept it clean, and most of its inhabitants were carried clear away into the ocean."

Some of the people fleeing to the hills called to a German merchant as they passed his door, saying: "Get your family out quickly, and run for your lives."

He shouted: "Go about your business, you want me to run away that you may steal my goods." He went in and barred his doors. Poor man! daring thieves on some former occasion had doubtless closed his ears against the timely warning of his friends. In a minute after, his house, with himself and family all locked in, was carried into the sea and crushed to pieces. They were seen no more. Severe earthquakes on this coast occur once in a hundred years, but a second destructive visitation of that sort within nine years is quite exceptional.

Pabellon de Pica is one of the great guano-loading ports of Peru. There are here and at Haunillos, 22 miles south, including a few vessels at Point Labos, one hundred and three ships. My work is to follow the currents of English commerce along the dark coasts of heathenism and of semi-Christian lands, to help to prevent the wreck of Christian character on those foreign reefs and rocks, and to secure those already wrecked, and to utilize men and money for missionary evangelizing purposes, instead of quietly allowing Satan to monopolize these resources and array them against the cause of God. Hence, it is quite in my line to enlist the men of the sea in this great work. I thought, possibly, I might arrange to send a man to labor in the hundred ships always to be found along the coast embracing these three great guano-loading stations. The difficulty of this undertaking is to find a man on the shore whom the captains and crews can trust with the funds they may be willing to give to initiate and support the work. Of course I was not acquainted with the few men residing on the shore, but supposing the captains to know them, I left that matter with them, and to select a secretary and treasurer whom they could trust.

I arrived in this port on Friday, the 25th of January. The surf was terrific; the roar and vibrations of the quaking earth occurred about every hour, day and night. I was baffled in my arrangement for a boat on Saturday, and did not get into the fleet till Sabbath morning. It was a gloomy prospect, but I hailed a ship's

boat that was passing, and asked them to put
me aboard the ship *Prince Umbertö*. I had
thought of trying to get the seamen together
in some central ship in the fleet and preach to
them, but as I ascended the ship's ladder, it
struck me, "Too late for that; better have informal services on as many ships as possible
for the captains, mates, and men of each ship."
Happy thought. I introduced myself to Captain Robert Scott, and he introduced me to his
wife and sister. I explained the object of my
visit, and showed the proposal I had written
in a little book for subscriptions, and said:
"Now, Captain, if it is your pleasure to call
your men aft, where they can get seats under the
awning, we will have an informal religious service, and then I will submit this matter to the
whole ship's company together."

"Very good," said he, and gave the order to
the mate to "call the men aft."

In about two minutes I had a congregation
of about twenty. Many of the men bare-foot-
ed, and in their shirt-sleeves, just as they were
at their ease, when called.

I said: "Men, I am glad to see you this
bright Sabbath morning. I am glad you
didn't get swallowed up by that big earth-

quake the other night. That would have been a bad job for some of us, wouldn't it? Well, this is not like Sunday at home, along with father, and mother, and sisters, still it is the Lord's blessed day of rest, and now I want you to join with me in singing His praise." I passed round and put a copy of "Hymns New and Old" into each sailor's hand. We'll sing the first hymn, "Oh for a thousand tongues to sing my great Redeemer's praise." They all joined in singing; those who knew the tune, and those who did not, all sang with a will. We then sang two or three others, among which was that sweet hymn, "What a friend we have in Jesus," from which I struck out and preached to them for half an hour about the sinner's Friend. The Holy Spirit manifestly touched many hearts. I am sure He touched mine, and filled it with love and sympathy for my dear seafaring brethren. We then united in prayer to God, and no service in Gothic structures could have been more solemn, for lo, God was in that place. I then stated to them my wish to send a man to labor in these fleets.

The captain said, "Men, if you wish to contribute, I will pay the amount you put down and keep account with you."

He then signed his name for 20 soles; the mates and men followed, and footed up the aggregate sum of 78 soles. The Captain ordered his men to send me to the ship *P. G. Carville*, Captain McFee; and I had a similar preaching service there.

3. In the ship *Ellersly*, Captain Mowat.

4. In the ship *Adria*, Captain Weiss.

5. In the ship *Herman*, Captain Dingle.

6. In the ship *Queen of the Mersey*, Captain Sinclair.

7. In the ship *Crosfield*, Captain Thompson.

Several captains had their families aboard. The singing in some of the ships was grand, and the services in all well received.

The next day, Captain Thomson, an earnest, Christian man accompanying, we had seven preaching services aboard of seven other ships. On Tuesday, the 29th of January, we had a meeting of the captains at the British Consulate, and adopted articles of agreement for the organization of a Seamen's Evangelical Society for the port of Pabellon de Pica. The following is a copy: "At a meeting of captains and other subscribers concurring in Rev. Wm. Taylor's proposal to send a preacher to labor in the port of Pabellon de Pica and vicinity, the following articles of agreement were unanimously passed :

I. That the two hundred and twenty-two subscribers to the fund be hereby constituted an association for the support of a minister of the Gospel, to labor among seamen in this port and vicinity.

II. That all future contributors to this fund shall thereby become members of this association.

III. That the captains of ships, being subscribers to the fund, shall, while at anchor in this port, be a committee to co-operate with the secretary, the treasurer, and the minister, in securing the object of this association.

It shall be the duty of the committee:

1st. To elect, and re-elect when necessary, a secretary and treasurer.

It shall be the duty of the secretary:

1st. To call a meeting of the committee, accompanied by a statement of the main object of the meeting, as occasion may require; after which general notice, five ship-masters meeting and voting, in conjunction with the secretary and treasurer, shall constitute a quorum for the transaction of business.

2d. To pay over immediately to the treasurer all funds coming into his hands for the association, except 200 soles to be kept in hand for incidental expenses.

3d. To keep an accurate record in a suitable book of all the official doings of the committee, and of all receipts and expenditures of the funds of the association.

It shall be the duty of the treasurer to deposit all the funds paid over to him in safe keeping, and pay it out only on checks signed by the secretary, and countersigned by two members of the committee.

It shall be the duty of the committee:

1st. To fix the amount to be paid monthly for the support of the preacher, at a rate not lower than £20 sterling, or its equivalent in currency, nor higher than £25 sterling per month. In case of the preacher's marriage, an additional sum to be allowed for family expenses, not exceeding in all £40 sterling per month, for himself and family.

2d. To select one or more of their number to go alone, or in company with the minister, as may seem best, to visit all the incoming ships, and inform the masters, mates, and men of this association, invite them to subscribe to its funds, and participate in its work.

3d. To designate a suitable vessel as Bethel

flag-ship, *pro tem.*, give due notice of the time of service, and invite their men to attend.

4th. To afford facilities aboard their ships on Sabbath days, or on week evenings, for informal services for singing, prayer, and preaching, and for the organization of Bible-reading classes and Christian fellowship bands, as the work may progress in a ship's company.

5th. To see that the funds of the association shall not be appropriated for the building of Bethels, nor for any other purpose than that for which they were contributed, viz.: the traveling expenses and support of the minister, and the incidental expenses necessarily incurred in the work.

Finally, the committee shall have power to change the location of the work, north or south on this coast, if required by change in the guano-loading ports.

Besides passing the foregoing articles of agreement, the meeting elected Mr. John Pennington as secretary, and Mr. East as treasurer, and an executive committee, as indicated in No. 3, to visit ships, etc., of which Captain Thompson, of the ship *Crosfield*, was the chairman.

The aggregate sum subscribed, meantime, amounted to 947 soles, worth about $600 in silver. The ships lie in that port from three to six months; no attractions on the land to entice the seamen, no land-sharks in those waters, a needy and grand field for service among the men of the sea. The captains and men felt the importance of the movement, and have subscribed cheerfully and liberally, but the weak point was the want of confidence for the security of their funds ashore. They offered to pay the money to me, but I was on the wing like themselves, and moreover did not wish to handle it. However that may turn out, a man of God will be duly sent to that needy field.

IX.

This guano-loading port, with a fleet of about fifty ships, is twenty-two miles distant from Pabellon de Pica. I came hither by the same little steamer, *Balistas*, on Wednesday, the 30th of January. Our cargo consisted principally of hay and blasting-powder.

"No smoking allowed on deck. There are a hundred barrels of powder all around you," shouted the captain. He could not command the sparks of the low smoke-stack of his steamer. I noticed that the head of the next barrel to the one on which I sat had been broken in, and thought, "well, one spark striking into that opening would relieve us of any further apprehension of earthquakes and tidal waves." On examination, however, I found that the powder was contained in a bag, and the bag was protected by the barrel. This was part of a cargo of powder from America

169

which arrived in Pabellon de Pica last Saturday. It was the boat of the powder-ship that conveyed me into the fleet at Pabellon last Sunday.

The captain says he was three hundred miles from land on the 23d instant, when the earthquake occurred. Said he: "I was lying down in my cabin reading, and was startled by a roaring sound and terrible pitching of the ship, and thought it an explosion of the powder. I rushed for the deck, expecting to see the ship in flames, but to my surprise and joy the ship was all right. Then I knew what it was, and thought of the peril of the people on the land."

We reached Huanillos just as the sun was beginning to dip into the western waters.

On the recommendation of two of my liberal subscribers and friends at Pabellon de Pica, Captain Edwards of the *True Briton*, and Captain Jones of the ship *Callao*, I hired a boatman on my arrival at Huanillos to pull me directly to the ship *Naval Reserve*, Captain Morgan, a Christian gentleman. I had but one day to devote to that great fleet of ships, or else be detained a week, which my work and limited time would not allow. So I prepared my subscription book and articles of agreement to be adopted at a meeting of captains, before I should leave, organizing an association similiar to that in Pabellon de Pica. It was too large an undertaking for one day, but I believed it possible, by the help of the Lord, and we, hence, proceeded with the work. We began Thursday morning with a service on the *Naval Reserve*. After the preaching, I explained the plan of sending a man of God to labor in the fleet, and Captain Morgan and his crew subscribed 102 soles. During the day we held nine services on nine different ships: the *Moss Rose*, Captain J. McNair; *Corsica*, of Glasgow, Captain A. Nichall; bark *Mary*, of Glasgow, Captain Thomas Davis; *Emma Ives;* ship *Governor Wilmore*, Captain G. P. Low; ship *British Empire*, Captain Riches; ship *Peter Young*, Captain Cain; ship *Eastern Light*, Captain Evan Jones. The captains, mates, and men of those ships, with great cheerfulness and good will, subscribed an aggregate sum of 592 soles, value nearly $400. We announced, as we went along, a meeting of captains to be held at the British Consulate at 5 P.M. We held our meeting accordingly, with about eighteen captains. The meeting adopted the articles of agreement to organize The Huanillos Seamen's Evangelical Society, and elected an executive committee, but could not agree on the selection of a resident secretary and treasurer, which seems essential, at least in the absence of a minister. If I had the right preacher on board, then we should be safe enough in all our arrangements. The captains hoped they might be able to arrange it in the fleet, transferring the books and money-box as each secretary and treasurer should sail. I don't yet know what they did, but the probability is that in the hurry of their business, the matter of completing the organization and collecting and depositing the funds would be postponed till the day of sailing, and then with no time left, they one by one would be off. So I hope against fear for both those fleets. I have not the slightest distrust of the men who subscribed. I know they would not willingly be parties à *farse* and a failure, but unless they could satisfy themselves of the safety of the fund subscribed, the only thing I should advise them to do would be to keep it in their own pockets. I did not receive a cent of it, though I perhaps made a mistake in not receiving sufficient for the passage of the men; still, if the Lord has the right men available, and I can find them, I must get the passage funds elsewhere, and send them. I have sufficiently prospected the field. I am safe in tying on to the seamen who do business in those waters, and I can't consent to a failure at all.

Thursday, 9 P.M., Captain Morgan took me in his boat to the steamship *Lima*, of the P. S. N. Co., on which I leave the coast of Peru. We steam along, and touch at the four ports of Bolivia.

1. Tocopilla, great copper mines and works. One hundred and twenty Cornishmen at work there, and no man to care for their souls. A few of them hold a meeting every Sabbath in a private house. I saw a few leading men, and proposed to send them a preacher, but could not stay to enlist sufficient interest to secure certainty of success.

2. Cobija,

3. Mejillones—two guano-loading ports.

4. Antofagasta, my next field for work.

X.

LANDED here Saturday A.M. the 2d of February. Was generously entertained by the P. S. N. Co.'s Agent, E. W. Foster, Esq., and his widowed mother. I was pleased to meet here an old friend from Australia, a genial gentleman, Dr. Neill, the physician of Antofagasta. The principal exports of this town, of about 10,000 population, are saltpeter, silver, and copper.

The great industries of the place are, first, extensive railway works, under the general supervision of George Hicks, Esq. Mr. Clemison has charge of the machine shops. There is a main line of railroad extending back seventy miles to Salinas, which with various branches makes an aggregate of about one hundred miles of railway, doing an immense business.

174

J. G. Adamson, Esq., has charge of the salt-peter works, which are of vast proportions.

John Tonkin, Esq., has charge of the silver-smelting works.

The "plant" of these silver works cost $450,000. They have been in operation four years. The yield of bar silver is in value about $300,000 per month. They have reached as high as half a million of dollars per month. The steam that has done its work in the silver smelting, and would be wasted, is utilized for condensing water for the use of the inhabitants of the town. Mr. Tonkin turns out 24,000 gallons per day, for which the people pay him seven cents per gallon. The following exhibit, by the favor of the British Consul of Antofagasta, H. R. Stevenson, Esq., will tell its own story about the Bolivian resources in this dry region. We present here the exports for the four last months of 1877, multiplied by three, giving approximately the exports for the past year, as follows :

Of saltpeter, 1,015,290 quintales, worth about $3 per quintale—$3,045,870.

Of silver, 446,250 marks, worth about $10 per mark,—$4,462,500.

Of copper, 52,800 quintales, worth about $2.50 per quintale—$132,000.

Making an aggregate mineral export value of $7,640,370.

All the men named are to my mind liberal, generous-hearted gentlemen, and most of the men employed by them seem to be a rough-and-ready, generous class of men. I made to them the following proposal:

Antofagasta being in need of a school, in which the children of English, German, and the better class Bolivian families may obtain a good English education, I propose to send a competent teacher to supply this demand.

As the residents, travelers, and seamen in this town would be benefited by religious services in the English language, I engage that the teacher shall be qualified to conduct them, and do the work of a pastor, religious creeds not to be interfered with nor taught in the school. It will require two hundred dollars to pay passage of the teacher hither, and at least one hundred dollars per month to support him. Passage funds will be required in April of this year, the other monthly, as the work shall progress. The school to be made self-supporting as soon as possible, and thus relieve the monthly subscribers.

"This agreement to cover a period of at least three years.

"Respectfully submitted,

"W. T.

"ANTOFAGASTA, February 2, 1878."

This was concurred in by forty-seven subscribers, with an aggregate subscription of four hundred and ninety-five dollars, instead of the two hundred asked, and one hundred and forty-five dollars monthly subscription, instead of one hundred.

This may illustrate the statement made by the people at all the places in which I have wrought on this coast: "There will be no difficulty about getting all the money you need here, if you can give us the right sort of men." I say to them, "I have no hope of finding men who can please everybody, but I expect, for each place, to find a man competent to perform all that his engagement requires—a man of God, who will do his duty conscientiously. You may not like him at first, but with patience and further acquaintance, you will find him to be the right man in the right place."

Among many new, cherished friendships formed during my brief sojourn in Antofagasta was an acquaintance with Señor Don E. Villena, Peruvian Consul for Bolivia. He was Peruvian Minister in Washington for some years, speaks our language well, and highly appreciates our country, its government, its schools, and its Gospel ministry for the intelligible instruction of the people. I have traveled in company with him many days, enjoyed his genial conversation, and got much valuable information from him in regard to his own country.

Took passage from Antofagasta on Wednesday noon, the 6th of February, for Caldera, Chile, in the P. S. N. Co.'s steamship *Potosi*. Owing to extraordinary tides in the harbor of Callao, sweeping away a great deal of property, and suspending all shipping business for a time, the *Potosi* was a day behind her time, and in consequence did not stop at Caldera; so I had to change at Chañaral to the steamer *Itata* of the Chile line.

The first mate of the *Itata*, George Burton, showed me great kindness. His father, Col. Burton of the Madras army, devoted many years of his life to Christian work as an evangelist. George is a noble, energetic fellow, and if converted to God, and called by the Spirit, would make a grand missionary.

Chañaral is the most northerly port of Chile. Our ship *Potosi* took aboard on this trip 250 tons of copper at this port. It is cast here into solid bars of 300 lbs. each.

The steam winch winds up a sling load of 1,200 lbs. every minute and a half—a very different process from the weighing and loading of these 300-lb. bars which I saw at the smelting works. Two men with great iron tong-claws clutch a bar and lay it on the scales. When weighed, two other men with their hands lay each bar on the shoulders of one of our burden - bearing cousins, who receives it in a kind of open knapsack, so adjusted as to divide the weight between the two shoulders and head a peculiar cap or band attached to the upper side of the sack passes round the forehead. In this Cousin Cholo carries a bar, and tumbles it into a railway car that conveys the cargo to the lighter which conveys it to the ship.

The manager of the copper smelting works informed me that the establishment cost two and a half millions of dollars. It was founded and owned ten years ago by our cousin Don Federica Varela, and sold by him in 1873 to the English company, to which it now belongs.

Chañaral has a population of 3,500, 1,200 of whom are miners. The total exports of this center of commerce for 1876 amounted in value to $4,581,855.

Chañaral was not on my list of places to be visited, and I had never heard of the place till I got nearly to it, but happily a young minister, Rev. Mr. Langbridge, and his wife, had arrived there from England but a month before, to teach and to preach, and had commenced their work with encouraging prospects of success.

The P. S. N. Co.'s agent in Chañaral received me with great cordiality. He is the son of a minister of the Scotch Kirk, who, as chaplain in the Indian army, resided many years in Bombay; hence the fact that I am a minister of the Gospel and a missionary from India allied him to me strongly. The Lord bless him and his family. I had a letter of commendation from the manager of the P. S. N. Co. for the Pacific Coast—Noel West, Esq.—to all his agents along my line of travel, and they all showed me great kindness, which I am glad to acknowledge; but such as had been in some way allied to missionary work were more especially affectionate in their attentions to me.

A Russian fellow-passenger on the *Itata* had seen me in Iquique, where he has a wife and two children. The poor fellow was suffering a recovery from a drunken debauch—a fine-looking, capable man. He took me into his room to tell me about his father and mother, now over eighty years old, who were daily praying for him, and writing him to come home and see them before they shall depart from this world.

He exclaimed many times, " Oh, this accursed drink! I shall never see my fader and mudder any more! I shall go down to hell! I can't quit; I try, but the very first day I meet some old friend who says, 'Come and take a drink.' He think me mean and stingy if I no drink with him, and I go and drink." I talked to him, and prayed for him, and while on my knees he got under the bunk, with his face on the floor, and roared in the agony of despair. Drinking and drunkenness have swept away thousands of such men on this coast, and not one teetotal minister of the Gospel between California and Valparaiso, a distance of six thousand miles. Dr. Trumbull and a few of his earnest men have lifted up the only total-abstinence flag that ever floated on this coast.

Never a country known in greater need of Christian workers than this West Coast of South America.

I have put a godly man and a stanch total abstainer in Callao, and by the grace of God we shall man this whole coast with them.

Let us thank God, and unite in singing,

"There's a better day a-coming."

P. S.—NEW YORK, June 20th, 1878.—I have appointed Prof. A. T. Jeffreys, B.A., according to the foregoing agreement, to labor as teacher and preacher in Antofagasta.

XI.

THE lower half of their national flag is red. The inner square of the upper half contains the great star, on a ground of blue; the remainder of the upper half of their flag is white. The tradition is cherished by our Chileno cousins, that their star belongs to the galaxy displayed on the national emblem of the "Great Republic." They are pleased thus to designate our nation, and to emulate us in all that pertains to good government and progress.

They commenced under great disabilities; they have passed through many revolutionary struggles; but for a long time past they have enjoyed peace and prosperity, and with a liberal provision for public instruction for the rising generation, increasing light, religious liberty, and an open Bible, they are bound to develop a grand nationality. But it cannot reasonably be expected that their growth can at any time be so rapid as that of any of our great States, even if the internal conditions essential to national growth were alike equal in both, for they have no such streams of foreign immigration as pour continually upon our shores.   In a population of 2,319,266 only 26,635 are set down as foreigners, and one-third of these belong to other South American States.   Seven hundred and seventy-eight are from North America.   There are from Europe 13,147 males and 3,828 females, making a total of Europeans amounting to 16,975, which are subdivided as follows: — Great Britain, 3,261 ; Germany, 2,926 ; France, 2,425 ; Italy, 1,670 ; Spain, 1,029 ; Portugal, 279 ; Austria, 203, and a sprinkling from seventy - two smaller nationalities.   It should be borne in mind, however, that by the laws of the commonwealth all the children of foreigners born in Chile are born to citizenship, and hence are not noted in the national census as foreigners. Most of the aforesaid 4,000 European and North American women are mothers, and many of them have large families.   Suppose they should each count an average of three children, we should then have 12,000 young people and children, who are not set down as foreigners ; and besides, from the 13,147 men, discounting from the census 3,000 as probable husbands of the aforesaid mothers, we have 10,000 men, from whom we may fairly presume there would be an offspring greatly exceeding 12,000 more, for a very large number of those men are married to native ladies, of every grade of society, from the highest to the lowest; so that the whole number of foreigners put down in the census, multiplied by three, will give, approximately, the numerical strength of the foreign element in the population of the State.

The total number of deaths in Chile for ten years, from 1865 to 1874, was 506,011. Of these 294,559—more than one-half—were under seven years of age, and were landed safely in heaven. The increase of population in that period was fourteen per centum. There are in Chile, according to the census, one hundred and one women for every one hundred men.

"In the beginning God made man male and female," and paired them in marriage union with each other, and through all the ages, and among all nations of men, He maintains His original plan of bringing them into the world, male and female, in about equal numbers of

each sex. The British Government, in the sup-
pression of the cruel infanticide of the Hin
dūs, by which millions of female babes have
been put to death by their parents, orders a
census of every suspected district yearly, and
if the male largely exceed in number the
female children, relying on this great law of
Providence, she proceeds at once to make
inquisition for blood, and executes summary
justice upon the guilty. In some countries
the equipoise of the two sexes is disturbed by
emigration, but that fact rather confirms than
contradicts the primal law. God thus in ac-
cordance with His written laws pertaining to
His institution of marriage maintains a standing protest against polygamy, adultery, and
every infringement of His provision for the
propagation and development of the human
race. When we remember that we are "the
offspring of God," and that "according to His
purpose" our probation in this world is simply
preparatory to a standing in the royal family
of heaven, heirs of God and joint heirs with
Jesus Christ "to an incorruptible inheritance,"
we need not wonder that God should reveal
the laws and maintain the government essential to a realization of His grand ideal of glori-

fied men and women; hence the dreadful con-
demnation and curse entailed by a violation of
God's laws pertaining to marriage, or the abuse
of any resource essential to the purposes of His
marriage institution.   The wickedness of such
sinners is not that they possess a sexual appe-
tite, which is common to the race, and within
the limitations of His laws as legitimate as
any other, but that they allow it to enslave
the noble attributes of their higher "soul and
spirit" nature, and, thus debased, proceed in
defiance of God to destroy the essential foundations of good society, and defeat the realization
of His grand purpose in giving life and being
to man, and in continuing his existence in the
world.

As an index to the industries of Chile, I
may mention that there are engaged in farm-
ing, mining, and merchandise 570,599 men and
316,146 women.

Professors in medicine and artists, 13,464
men and 5,550 women.

Journalists and writers, 7,354 men.

Sailors, 4,724; and soldiers, 6,838.

As far back as 1850, under the administration of President Mont, the government initi-
ated, and has ever since been developing, a free-

school system of different grades, drawing its support from the national treasury, to the annual amount of about $800,000.

Nothing worthy of note has been done to found English schools in Chile, except in Valparaiso, the Athens of the Republic. Rev. Dr. Trumbull and his friends founded a good English school in that city about a quarter of a century ago, which under the able management of Prof. Mackay has done a great educational work for the country. Many other schools there, also, have contributed to supply the growing demand of the people for education, among which is a good German school, under the direction of an able German Protestant minister.

The climate of Chile in excellence cannot be surpassed in any part of the world, and is equaled only by that of California.

In agriculture, its productions of wheat, barley, oats, and other cereals and vegetables correspond in quality with the same products in California, but not quite equal in quantity per acre. Its fruits, too, in variety and quality, correspond with the fruits of the Golden State.

The following table of Chilean exports, extending from 1844 to 1875, will convey an idea of the variety and relative values of their products. This is for the eye of the statistician, and hence the common reader may skip it, and pass on.

CLASSIFICATION.	VALUATION.
Wheat, ...	$61,830,650
Flour, ...	51,726,391
Barley, ...	16,421,646
Hides, ...	10,536,475
Wool, ...	10,099,635
Timber, ...	5,261,749
Cattle, ...	3,321,784
Leather, ...	2,938,810
Jerk beef, ...	2,872,932
Beans, ...	2,646,581
Potatoes, ...	2,394,178
Nuts, ...	2,091,742
Honey, ...	1,549,543
Hay, ...	1,263,062
Sheep, Mules, and Horses, . .	1,252,630
Salt Meat, ...	1,181,588
Linseed, ...	1,128,915
Bran, ...	1,106,516
Cheese, ...	1,067,927
Butter, ...	867,434
Lard, ...	808,430
Beeswax, ...	745,015
Common Grease, ...	702,080
Indian Corn, ...	501,597
Cascara Bark, ...	350,795
Total, ...	$184,668,108

The Cáscara bark is used for making a cleansing and medicinal wash for the skin.

Mineral products in Chile, minus the large yield of gold, correspond with those of California, with such an excess of copper over any other country as to supply, until within a few years, two-thirds of the whole demand of the markets of the world. Her supply is exhaustless, but the competition of Wisconsin and of South Australia has sadly depreciated its market value.

The following table of the export of the mineral products of Chile, from 1844 to 1875, I insert simply for those specially interested in statistics :

Bar Copper,	$155,077,806
Copper, partly smelted,	84,515,195
Copper Ore,	33,553,903
Half-smelted Silver and Copper,	13,189,958
Bar Silver,	71,544,629
Silver and Gold Coin,	21,263,964
Silver Ore,	15,708,542
Gold Dust,	2,017,164
Stone Coal,	6,089,632
Total,	$402,960,793

The following table of Chilean imports from foreign countries will tell its own story:

Sources of Supply for 1875 and 1876.		Increase.	Diminution for '76
England . . .	$15,702,808	$12,625,728	. . . .	$3,077,080
France	7,814,811	7,503,498	. . . .	311.313
Germany . . .	4,162,138	3,729,651	. . . .	432,487
Argentina . .	2,727,262	3,097,736	$370,474	. . . .
United States.	2,133,443	2,626,055	492,612	. . . .
Peru	2,410,637	2,480,323	69,686	. . . .
Belgium . . .	786,804	740,444	. . . .	46,360
Spain	329,879	733,855	403,976	. . . .
Brazil	492,776	478,320	. . . .	14,456
Italy	283,015	453,168	170,153	. . . .
Ecuador . . .	198,615	254,311	55,696	. . . .
Uruguay . . .	98,780	115,464	16,684	. . . .
Cent. America	133,098	96,548	. . . .	36,550
India	. . . .	62.613	62,613	. . . .
Portugal . . .	56,250	61,307	5,057	. . . .
Bolivia	578,456	55,522	. . . .	522,934
Polynesia . . .	57,394	28,218	. . . .	29.176
Paraguay . . .	39,088	25,080	. . . .	14,008
China	15,989	6,238	. . . .	9,751
Colombia . . .	25,316	. . . .	. . . .	25,316
Undesignated.	90,941	116,962	26,021	. . . .
Total. . . .	$38,137,500	$35,291,041	$1,672,972	$4,519,431
Diminution in 1876				$2,846,459

So you may see that our cousins, in this salubrious climate, enjoy the good things of other nations, and are willing to pay a fair price for them; but for a few years past, in common with the rest of mankind, they have been spending too freely, and now they are curtailing expenses. May our fair cousins pardon me, if I suggest that they could help to relieve the exchequer of their husbands or fathers if they should put into their skirts a few yards less of foreign silks and satins, or else not fray them out by trailing them along the dusty streets; and then it would be such a relief to pedestrians. To come within the sweep of a lot of the beautiful creatures of a dry day, why you might as well encounter a small whirlwind on a dusty plain.

I am aware that ordinary readers do not relish statistics, and find them very indigestible, but such will pardon me for setting before them another dish of the dry things, for the pleasure of those who like them. We are not bound to eat every thing that is set before us.

There is a story told of an Indian chief in Oregon who was invited to dine with a colonel in the United States Army, and took note of the number of courses served at the table of his host. Soon after he invited the colonel to dine with him. The first course was roast horse. After they had partaken pretty freely, the chief gave orders to his servant, saying:

"Take him off." After the due interval he said : "Fetch him on again," and it was "take him off and fetch him on" till the full number of his white brother had been served, but it was roast horse all through; not so with my courses of statistics.

The following is an exhibit of Chilean exports to foreign markets.

Nations receiving in 1875 and 1876.		Increase.	Decrease for 1876.
England . . .	$21,033,490 $21,380,322	$346,832	. . .
France	3,006,850 4,449,866	1,443,016	. . .
Peru	5,441,641 4,449,923	. . .	$991,718
Bolivia	2,228,875 2,429,701	140,826	. . .
United States	417,816 1,085,602	667,786	. . .
Germany . . .	927,810 1,066,509	138,699	. . .
Uruguay . . .	1,176,286 746,383	. . .	429,30
Argentina. . .	421,314 474,579	233,265	. . .
Ecuador . . .	175,728 326,677	150,949	. . .
Brazil	286,234 281,984	. . .	4,250
Cent. America	77,568 195,142	117,574	. . .
Colombia . . .	54,286 109,171	54,885	. . .
Polinesia . . .	100,164 89,133	. . .	11,031
Portugal . . .	2,668 2,085	. . .	583
Cuba	. . . 1,300	1,300	. . .
Mexico	12,006 1,000	. . .	11,006
Australia . . .	19,966 . . .	. . .	19,996
Belgium . . .	1,754 . . .	. . .	1,754
Unnamed . . .	663,136 681,762	18,632	. . .
Total	$35,927,592 $37,771,139	$3,335,145	$1,491,598

Increase for the year 1876, ... $1,843,547

Chile has a standing army of 3,000 men, with

a national guard of 25,000, and a navy of ten steamships, manned by 450 men. The Chilean statistics I have inserted may serve as an illustrative sample of the international commercial relations of all the Republics of South America, and of the Empire of Brazil as well. It seems a pity that their commerce with "the Great Republic" is so small, but it is owing to no fault of our cousins. Like everybody else, they have to buy and sell where they can do the best for themselves; but they are anxious for a closer alliance with us, and we should appreciate and love them more than we have hitherto done. May the Lord cause His face to shine upon them, and bless them.

XII.

CALDERA.

THIS is a town of twelve hundred inhabitants, of whom 157 are English, 27 North Americans, and 76 Germans. It is the port of entry for a vast silver-mining district. Its commercial importance may be perceived by a glance at the footings of a single column of her statistics. Total of sail vessels that cleared from this port in 1876 were 154, with an aggregate tonnage 61,783; steamers 298, with a tonnage 306,941. Only about half the sail vessels were destined to foreign ports. The same steamers, about sixty in number, touch here many times in the year.

J. C. Morong, Esq., the American Consul at Caldera, a prominent merchant of the town, is a gentleman worthy of a hundred times more commercial business than our marine service has ever furnished him. I found a very hospitable home at his house during my brief sojourn in Caldera.

There were more English-speaking people here
a quarter of a century ago than now, but they
have never had English preaching, except once
in a few years a preacher happened to spend
a Sabbath in passing.   Naturally enough, the
most of the people have lost nearly all relish
for such things, but are nevertheless kindly
disposed toward good men, and would be glad
to have an English school.   In consultation
with Mr. Morong, Mr. Jacques, manager of the
railway works of Caldera, and Mr. Jack, the
British Consul for that port, it was agreed that
the Consul should issue a circular, calling a
meeting of the leading citizens for that night,
Friday, the 8th of February.   Mr. Jack kindly
introduced me to most of the English-speaking
families, and we tried to prepare their minds
for the work contemplated.   About fifteen or
more attended the meeting, which was held in
the parlor of a beer saloon, for the reason, it
was alleged, that the people would be more
likely to assemble there than in a private
family parlor.   The landlord, of course, was
very attentive and kind.   No one patronized
his bar while I remained, but what they did
in gratitude for his kindness after I left, I cannot say.   I only know that the ardor I had

succeeded in kindling in some hearts for the reception of a man of God to teach their chil- ren and preach to the people, had abated con- siderably by the next morning. I, however, visited a few families, and was teaching some children to sing, and could have turned the tide that day and made a success, but receiving a letter of invitation from Mr. John Rosser and Richard · Tonkin to spend the Sabbath in Copiapo, I thought it my duty to take the train that morning in response to their call. A Rev. Mr. Sayre had served the Copiapo people for a year or two, but went to America about two years since, so I would not go to that field till I could learn certainly that Mr. Sayre did not intend to return to it, and that the people were not in negotiation for any other minister. So, on arrival, I got Mr. Morong to write Mr. Rosser, and I wrote Mr. Tonkin. Their prompt answer was that the coast was all clear, and they were anxious to have me visit them. I had offered my services for Sabbath in Caldera at our meeting last night, but no motion was made for or against my preaching to them, which I should have taken the responsibility of doing in some shape, had I not received this call to Copiapo. So the people of Caldera were left to their reflections till the following Wednesday A.M., when I returned from Copiapo. Having to take steamer that afternoon for Valparaiso, I had but a few hours to spend with them. I was very sorry, for the dear neglected people of Caldera need help, and it is a hopeful field. There would be no difficulty in raising a school of thirty scholars of the English-speaking, and it was asserted confidently by old residents that the better class natives would patronize it largely. Accompanied by an earnest railway engineer, I spent my few remaining hours in calling on the people for their pledges in subscription to bring out a man, and nearly the amount required was put down on our paper. So I left the work in the hands of my earnest engineer.

A few weeks later, on my return north, I made a hasty visit ashore while our ship was discharging Caldera freights, and found that they had obtained pledges sufficient to bring out a single man, and that a number of native families wished to share in the enterprise, but specially desired a female teacher for their daughters. The general conclusion then was that anything short of a man and his wife, both competent teachers, would not fill the bill. I hope they will succeed, but in attempting too much at once, they may fail in that which is quite practicable. Their desire, however, is not in excess of their need, nor of the resources of the school to support a man and his wife adequately, being first-class teachers; and I don't propose nor intend to send any who are not first-class; but the only hitch is the want of a small amount of ready money to pay their passage hither.

P. S.—NEW YORK, June 21, 1878.—Have not yet heard from Caldera, but have already ordered school furniture for that with the rest of the places, and expect to send them teachers before the year is out, if the Lord will have it so, and I believe that to be His purpose.

XIII.

COPIAPO.

FOR more than a quarter of a century this has been the central resort of the silver miners and traders, attracted to this region by the rich silver mines in this district. It has a population of about 20,000, of whom there are 157 English, 27 North American, and 76 Germans. There are in this town and vicinity many Cornish miners, as indeed in the mining region of this and all other countries. A very large proportion of these are traditionally Wesleyans. Not many of them show signs of spiritual life now. A fossil will remain the same in any country. It is a dead, unfeeling thing, and can't appreciate moisture, nutrition, and cultivation, so essential to life. But a Cornish Christian has a religion of sap and joyous emotion. He must assemble with the saints, and with them sing and shout the

praises of God. He must sit "under the drop-
pings of the sanctuary," and be well watered,
or he will wither and die. "Planted by the
rivers of water, he is an evergreen; will bring
'forth his fruit in his season,' and abide forever." But plant such a man down in this
great "Atacama desert," which has not been
watered since the days of Noah, and he dies.

If ministers of God had come with them, as
they should have done, and opened the wells
of salvation along this coast, we should now
behold everywhere streams in the desert and
the country, foreign and native alike, set with
fruitful trees of righteousness planted by the
Lord; too much "red tape" binds unduly the
home church organizations.

We have this vision verified in a small de-
gree here in Copiapo. A few years ago an
earnest Cornish blacksmith by the name of
Uhren went to work and got his people together, sang to them the hymns they used
to hear in Gwenep pit, and preached the Gospel to them. Many were revived, a Sunday-
school was commenced, and although Brother
Uhren went away to California years ago, regular preaching services and the Sunday-school
have been kept up ever since. To be sure, two

9*

missionaries in succession have spent a few years here since this work was commenced, affording them some help, but devoting their time principally to the natives. But the Cornish work, conducted by laymen before the missionaries came and went, has kept steadily on its way. John Rosser, Richard Tonkin, and Thomas Mitchell are the present leaders of the movement.

On the invitation of Bros. Tonkin and Rosser I came on Saturday by rail, forty miles, from Caldera to Copiapo, and remained three days. On Sabbath A. M. and night I preached to the people, and addressed the Sunday-school of about thirty in the afternoon. On each occasion their room for worship was crowded inside with English people and a sprinkling of natives, with a greater crowd of natives about the doors and windows. After preaching in the evening we had a meeting to consider the question of having me send them a minister. Mining here is very dull now, and the people, both in numbers and ability, have been reduced by one-half within a few years, and hence they have only half the ability for assuming such a responsibility as they formerly had. The same is true all along the coast. But the need of the people and their desires are such that they entered into an agreement to raise the funds requisite, and requested me to send two teachers, a man and his wife, to found a male and female school, the man to be their pastor as well. It is a very heavy lift for them, but all together they can do it.

Copiapo is one of the principal towns of the province of Atacama. The whole province contains a population of 69,000 natives, 547 English, and 52 Americans. The desert of Atacama extends far into Bolivia and Peru. Copiapo has a small river from the mountains passing through it, hence surrounded by farms, orchards, vineyards, ornamental shrubbery and flowers. It is indeed an oasis literally, as it is in religious interest and organization. It has a large and beautiful plaza, densely shaded with pepper-trees, not a useful variety of pepper, but grandly suited to the purpose for which it is used. A plaza with a fountain, shrubbery, and flowers is an essential in the make-up of a South American town. Even in Antofagasta, where water costs seven cents per gallon, they have their fountain and shrubbery and floral garden.

XIV.

This is the next port south of Caldera, and the principal commercial center of the province of Coquimbo.

The population of the province is officially put down at 58,000, over 800 of whom are English. The city of Coquimbo contains 12,650 inhabitants; 23 are set down as North Americans, and 416 as English.

The city of Serena, nine miles distant, has a population of 29,000 thousand. Ovalle, forty miles away by railroad, has 4,000. There are many Cornish and Welsh miners in this province. Nearly all these eight hundred foreigners speak the Spanish language, and this is the native language of their children born in this country—a body of agency sufficient to reflect the light of a pure Gospel to all the native denizens of this province, if they themselves were saved and endowed with the pentecostal power of the Holy Spirit.

The value of exports from Coquimbo for 1876 aggregates the amount of $15,989,263.

In the same time there were cleared from this port 479 sail vessels, with a total registry of 93,186 tons; steamers, 498, tonnage, 498,360. These figures represent both the foreign and coast trade. Many of the same vessels on the coast trade, especially the steamers, have been cleared many times during the year. I have simply selected from elaborate tables of statistics a few index facts to give an idea of the importance of Coquimbo as a center for evangelistic work.

About one hundred and sixty-nine Welsh and Cornish people, besides a few natives, live at Guayacan, nearly two miles distant from Coquimbo.

Thomas Francis, the manager of the extensive copper smelting works there, is also a sort of bishop of the town, and has for many years kept up religious services, and kept up also among the people the habit of a regular attendance at the house of the Lord. I addressed his large Sunday-school on Sabbath P.M., the 24th of March, and preached in his chapel that night. The place was crowded with attentive hearers. They have had a minister for about four

years past—Rev. Mr. Jones, a Welsh Presbyterian. He taught school week-days and
preached on the Sabbath—the only English-
speaking minister for years past between
Valparaiso and Callao, a distance of 1,500
miles.

Not wishing in any way to interfere with
this dear brother's work, I did not expect to attempt anything, even in Coquimbo, and hence,
on my southward voyage, did not tarry here.
But on my return north, Brother Jones met
me at the ship, and begged me to do what I
could for Coquimbo, as he had arranged to sail
for England the 26th of April.

So I stopped a couple of days, and made
arrangements with the leading people of Coquimbo to supply them with a minister of the
Gospel, to devote his whole time to preaching
and pastoral work for that city and the towns
adjacent. The funds for passage, and over
$1,000 toward his support, were subscribed
before I left, and a committee organized to proceed with the work.

Captain Grierson, English and American
Consul, gave me valuable help. My home
was in the family of Mr. Robert John. I
found the people very home-like and kind,

and was sorry to part with them, but expect, the Lord willing, to see them again.

A sad occurrence cast gloom over the minds of the people during my short sojourn with them. A well-known and much-respected watchmaker and jeweler, by the name of Williams, was traveling on horseback in the night, near Serena City, where he lived, and was found dead by the roadside in the morning, his head badly bruised. It was supposed that he was thrown from his horse. He leaves a wife and eight or nine children to mourn his loss.

He belonged to the fraternity of Freemasons. About one hundred and fifty persons attended his funeral; a large number of them were natives belonging to the order. Rev. Mr. Jones read a funeral service, followed by the Masonic funeral ceremonies. One English and two native gentlemen delivered addresses on the occasion. The ceremony was closed by a native, whose last utterance was, " Adios, hermano, Weelyams, adios."

The Freemasons have lodges in all towns of note on this coast, among which are many native lodges, though interdicted by their padrés.

P. S. — NEW YORK, June 6th. — Passage money has been duly forwarded by the Secretary of our Committee, Thomas J. W. Millie, Esq.; and I have appointed Rev. J. W. Higgins, B.A., as pastor of Coquimbo and neighboring cities. He will, D. V., set sail from this city for his important field of labor on the 29th instant.

XV.

VALPARAISO.

This is the great commercial emporium of Chile. It is a city set on more than "seven hills" and precipitous bluffs facing the ocean. The hills are in semi-circular position, corresponding with the curve of the bay. The city has but two or three level streets; but these are furnished with "lower and upper deck" street cars, on which we can traverse its whole length. This level land, on which stand all the public buildings and most of the business houses, was mainly recovered from the sea. Many years ago, as I was told here on my way to California, the ocean made a desperate effort to repossess its old claims. It sent out a tremendous tidal wave, which carried a number of ships into this part of the city. They were laid up high and dry, but the great waters retired, and our cousins have held an undisputed right to the soil ever since. The great

tidal waves of 1868 and of 1877, which
wrought such devastation in Peru, did not
trouble this city; and the great blocks of
two and three story warehouses and stores,
all along these level streets, seem to be indif-
ferent alike to tidal waves and earthquakes.
Most of the dwellings and the school-houses
are located on the hills, many of them on
narrow terraces dug out irregularly along the
brow of the precipitous bluffs. We reach
these partly by ascending steep zigzag paths,
and partly by climbing long flights of stone
steps. A night view of the city from the
harbor, when all the dwellings on these cir-
cling hills are lighted with gas or kerosene, is
exquisitely beautiful.

By previous invitation, I enjoyed a welcome
happy home at the residence of Rev. D. Trumbull, D.D. The Doctor and his accomplished
lady and family received and treated me as a
brother beloved, and laid me under lasting
obligations by their great kindness. When I
preached for Dr. Trumbull in this city, nearly
thirty years ago, he was an unmarried, ruddy,
youthful-looking man, residing in the family of
Mr. Wheelwright, the founder of the P. S. N.
Co. I remember my surprise at that time

when Mr. Wheelwright told me of the number and tonnage of the steamships which had for several years been plying regularly from this city along the coast for 3,000 miles to Panama. Dr. Trumbull, though venerable in years, of rich experience, and grand achievement as a Christian minister, is still young in appearance, and sprightly as a college Freshman. His wife, who in abounding works of mercy has been climbing these hills for more than a quarter of a century, has become very corpulent, but is unceasing in trying to make everybody about her happy, and hence seems always to walk in the bright sunlight of happiness herself. They have four daughters, with one adopted, making five, and they treat all alike. Two of their daughters and their two sons are receiving their education in New Haven, Connecticut.

The parents are giving a liberal education to their children with the hope that they will use it all for God, in the further development of His work in the Republic of Chile. Their adopted daughter is married to a most loving Christian gentleman, Mr. Gomien. The Doctor, in addition to all his varied educational and pastoral work, is editor and publisher of a

monthly periodical, a royal octavo of sixteen
pages—*The Record;* also a similar one in the
Spanish language—*The Piedra.* Both are gra-
tuitously circulated, but are supported by the
voluntary donations of friends. The history of
Dr. Trumbull's years of toil here is nearly iden-
tical with the history of the reformed type of
Christianity in Chile. ·

At an annual meeting of the Union Church
Society, held on the 31st of last October, Dr.
Trumbull gave an historical summary of the
work in connection with his Union Church,
which I copy from the *Record* of November
16, 1877:

"The society has passed to a corporate,
chartered form. It has been recognized by the
Supreme Government and for the first time
legalized. It will be a fitting occasion for re-
cording some of the more salient points of our
history.

"In 1844 a request was forwarded to New
York that a minister might come to this city
to gather a congregation of English and American residents and seafaring men. The English Consular Chaplaincy had been established nine years previous. With a hope of
benefiting foreigners, as well as of ultimately

reaching by such means the native population, a society called the *Foreign Evangelical* took up this request, offering their commission just as I was terminating my studies in preparation for the ministry. I had asked to be guided in selecting a field of Christian effort, and considered the indication providential. Being ordained for the ministry in Valparaiso in June, 1845, I sailed in August, and arrived here on the 25th of December, Christmas Day.

."The prospect was anything but encouraging. It was impossible for six months to secure a room for a chapel, until at last we obtained a dark and diminutive bodega in the Quebrada Almendro. At the end of a month, however, the dining-room of the Chile Hotel was offered, which was commodious for an audience of a hundred. At the .end of a year orders came from the owners in Santiago to vacate the place on religious grounds. Ere another location could be had months elapsed, but we were allowed to remain, until at last we were settled for six or seven years at 24 Calle Aduana. In 1854, returning to the Quebrada and finding the bodega too strait for the congregation, we resolved to subscribe funds to buy land and build. The task seemed herculean, first to obtain the means, and next to get permission. The result, however, was that in April, 1856, the church we now call the old one—that sold to the Germans—was dedicated to the worship of God, the first Protestant church that was ever erected on the West Coast of Spanish America, from California to Cape Horn. We had to erect a board fence twelve feet high in front of it.

" When the land was purchased, a question arose as to how the title should be vested; and a legal friend (Dr. Alberdi) advised naming as trustees, or fideicomisarios, the British and American Consuls and others. In 1869 that building had become too small, and the present edifice in Calle San Juan de Dios was provided.

"The land of that first church built in 1855 cost $7,500, and the edifice $8,000; of this the American Seamen's Friend Society gave $1,000, and the rest was given here. The Society immediately became self-supporting.

" In 1864 the Union Hall was provided for Sunday-school and Union meetings, at a cost of $13,000.

" Four years later, in 1868, the assistance of

the Rev. Mr. Guy was secured as co-pastor, until his decease, which occurred five years later, in 1873.

"The present church, built in 1869, cost for land $26,000, and for the building $31,000. On this day our indebtedness is $6,000.

"While we may claim the credit of having been the first to build and occupy a church in opposition to an intolerant law of the republic, the Anglican congregation was formed first. It has also recently been in advance of us in active and successful measures to secure incorporation. In securing our charter, we had little to do beyond adapting their statutes to our rules and methods. The government in Santiago, without suggesting a single alteration, passed the statutes as they were presented.

"At the close of thirty-two years it may be added that, while we have here assembled, gathered from different portions of the earth, and differing nationally as well as denominationally, yet a remarkable measure of harmony has characterized our history. And if the past has not proved a failure, there is no reason to apprehend a less measure of success in the future. The principles of our fathers have been crowned

with good results during a score and a half of
years, and they require nothing but energy
and consistency on 'our part to have them
serve the same purpose for a century. ' We
personally may pass away, but others will rise
up to take our places.

"Another peculiarity of this congregation
has been the frequency of the changes taking
place in it. There may not be ten persons
connected with it to-day who belonged to it
thirty years ago. Often, as soon as persons have
come to be interested, they have moved away.
Although this has in it a measure of discour-
agement, still it has an advantage; the influence of the church is felt by a larger number
than could be the case in a more stationary
community. I judge that 2,500 persons have
been connected with the congregation from
the first day until now, 600 belonging to it at
the present time; while the number of com-
municants during the same period will have
ranged between 400 and 500 : to-day 150 are
upon the roll. From these facts the importance of our enterprise is evident to all. This
society occupies a position that can be made
one of widely extending influence. It stands
at a point where there is an ebb and flow

People come and depart. It is for us to cast our bread ofttimes upon the waters; we shall find it after many days."

I will here insert an additional chapter of history from the pen of Dr. Trumbull:

THE EPISCOPAL CHURCH.

"Having given in the last number of the *Record* a notice of the growth of the Union congregation from its first beginning, we have been requested to furnish some items bearing on the more general subject of the development here of the Protestant interest, and take up the pen now to answer this friendly suggestion.

"In 1823 the Protestant Cemetery was provided. Land was then bought and inclosed. There were at the period a larger number of Protestants resident than one might have supposed. In that year twenty-four subscribers gave $1,138 for the object; of these subscriptions, two only were from commercial firms.

"In 1823 an attempt was made by two Congregational missionaries from Boston, Rev. Messrs. Parvin and Brigham, to inaugurate evangelical work here under the American

10

Board, but for some unfortunate reason they became disheartened and relinquished the task as impossible or else desperate within a year or two.

"In 1825 a Mr. Kendall is reported to have conducted the Anglican worship at the house of the British Consul; for how long time is not quite certain, but the deceased Mrs. Fromont said that when she arrived here, in 1828, her husband rented the house which Mr. Kendall had just vacated on leaving the country.

"After that Mr. Sewell, a merchant, used to read prayers at a private house on the Cerro Alegre, until 1837, when the Rev. John Rowlandson, private tutor in the family of the late Richard Price, Esq., being a presbyter of the Church of England, was requested to commence regularly the services of the Church of England. His term of pastorate seems to have been about two years. Existing records show a marriage, No. 1, solemnized by him, July 5th, 1838, and another, No. 7, June 20th, 1839; but none later. The first baptism on record by Mr. R. is dated December 17th, 1837, and the last June 23d, 1839. Twenty baptisms then are entered, nineteen of them administered

by the Rev. Alexander Hy. Small, B. D., chap-
lain of H.B.M.S. *President*, and one by Hy. W.
Rouse, Esq., H.B.M.S. Consul; ranging from
July 28th, 1839, to April 23d, 1841.

"At that period the Rev. William Armstrong came to Valparaiso; he remained ten
years. Chilian ladies, married with Englishmen during his time, attempted to attend service in the English Church, and were notified
by the authorities that it could not be per-
mitted.

"The service was held in a chapel far up on
the Cerro Alegre, in a hall attached to a private
residence. The Union congregation, called
then at first the Free Chapel, was gathered in
1846, likewise in a private dwelling. The law
did not allow the public worship of dissenters.
When Mr. Armstrong left in April, 1852, the
Rev. Benjamin Hill succeeded him until April,
1856, when the Rev. Richard Dennett entered
on the duty as chaplain, performing it (save
an interval of nine months, during which the
Rev. John Buncher served as his substitute in
1867) until the end of 1869. The Rev. Wm.
H. Lloyd, the present incumbent, became pastor
in 1870. During his absence the Rev. W. B.
Keer officiates.

"In 1858 the present English church was erected. It drew the angry fire of the Archbishop in Santiago, who protested to the government against the infraction of the Constitution; his friends of the laity petitioning the President to have the edifice 'razed from the surface of the republic which it dishonored.' This firing was perfectly harmless. It had no effect, unless it were by recoil, for in 1865 the article of the Constitution on which the prelate sought to impale the administration was explained away, and so interpreted as to allow Protestants to have as many churches for public worship as they might choose.

"From this historic sketch one or two valuable points merit attention :

" 1. The first form of religious liberty that was obtained in this country for those not Roman Catholics was connected with the burial of the dead. That amount of freedom had to be granted from the moment when Spanish restrictions were removed and Protestants allowed and invited to come hither to reside.

" 2. The first effective attempt to care for the religious welfare of foreign Protestants living in this city was made by adherents of the Church of England. Parliament at that period aided by law in the support of Anglican chaplains in foreign parts, and by that benign provision helped pious men to care for Scotsmen, Englishmen, Germans, and Americans who were scattered as sheep without a shepherd on this coast.

" 3. The history of the Protestant enterprise in this part of the world shows that one successful method of securing religious freedom has been to go forward and assert it. By taking it, Protestants have secured it. Burials, baptisms, marriages, and gatherings for worship in chapels and churches may all have been illegal enough at one time, because in dissent from the majority of the inhabitants of Chile; but as the number of persons claiming these rights has augmented, and through courage, become respectable, they have come to be respected, until finally public opinion and national legislation are at one in guaranteeing religious liberty to all.

" There is only one point remaining in this connection now to the dishonor of the lawmakers of Chile, and the annoyance of the people, and that is the disability laid, in obedience to the demands of the Roman

Church, on men and women about contracting lawful marriages when not of the same creed. Let this be provided for, and the country will, legally at least, be free."

The disability is that if one party is a Roman Catholic, the other must become one also, unless by special permission of the Pope, which is expensive, and involves the obligation of training the children to be Roman Catholics. Even when both parties are Protestants they can only be legally married by a Roman Catholic priest.

The "Episcopal Church," thus early planted in Valparaiso, was not by the Protestant Episcopal Church of the United States, but by the Mother—the Established—Church of England, which, though suffering from fossilization, and from internal strifes and divisions, excels all other churches in her arrangements for appointing ministers to needy outposts of the earth. The Methodist Episcopal Church, in common with others, has two methods of extending her work into new fields: the one is a consecutive advance of the regularly organized work; remote, needy fields, as in South India and in South America, are entirely beyond the radius of this method: the other is by order of the "Mission Committee;" but the neglected people of those remote coasts are neither paupers nor heathens, and hence don't come within the jurisdiction of the Committee on Foreign Missions. But the "Church of England" never seems to have any difficulty in appointing a clergyman to any place on this planet, where his services are called for; and until very recently the government made liberal appropriations of money to subsidize any subscription of funds from any part of the world accompanied by a call for a minister. Hence, in nearly all parts of the earth, where there is an English community sufficient to support a blacksmith shop and keep up a post-office, we will find a clergyman of this Church, doing good in his way, though not generally very spiritual, as seen from our standpoint, and will by all possible means preclude from his field any minister who represents what he is pleased to call "a sect."

Among many charitable institutions in this city, both of English and German residents, I will only insert a notice of one for the distribution of the Holy Scriptures and other religious books. Their agent, Mr. Müller, is a German, and was converted to God in his "Fader-

land," through the agency of the founder of
Methodism in that land, Mr. Jacoby. Bro.
Müller speaks English and Spanish fluently,
and is an earnest Christian worker. The following notice will convey an idea of what is
being done to scatter leaves from the tree of
life for the healing of the nation:

BIBLE SOCIETY.

The Valparaiso Bible Society has just celebrated its seventeenth annual meeting. The
total sale of Scriptures during the year terminating January 31st, 1878, has been upward of
1,670 copies. Of these more than 200 have
been Spanish Bibles, 550 Spanish Testaments,
and 593 Gospels. English and German, French
and Swedish Scriptures have also been circulated through its agency.

Respecting other volumes, the aim is to distribute such as may serve to call attention to
the Holy Scriptures, or to explain and enforce
the truths revealed in them. The total distribution of books, not including the Scriptures,
has been upward of 3,600. Of these the larger
portion have been books in English, something
more than 1,800 in all; though upward of
1,500 Spanish books have been circulated. Con-

sidering how few suitable volumes have been published in Spanish, adapted to the use and aims of the society, this is not an unsatisfactory account.

Of German Scriptures we have to notice sale of 45 copies; of volumes in German, 177.

The total sales during the twelve months, in money value, have amounted to upward of $3,000.

The subscriptions for the year have been $2,500.

Valparaiso contains a population of about 80,000. It is the great commercial emporium of Chile. The number of sailing vessels entered in this port for the year 1876 was 784; and of steamers, 449, representing an aggregate capacity of 815,139 tons. It should be observed that many of the same vessels, especially of the steamships, are entered a number of times during the year.

The number of passengers arriving in this port during the year 1876 was 20,278; departures, 17,849, showing a gain of 2,429. Arrivals in 1877 were 19,317; departures, 15,133; excess of arrivals, 4,186.

10*

XV.

THIS noted whale - fishing station is 240 miles south of Valparaiso. I arrived on Friday, the 22d of February.

The whale-catching business here, as everywhere else, has greatly diminished, though some are still taken in these waters, and I saw a few the day before my arrival here that have not been caught yet, but they are scarce and hard to catch; and now that we can strike rivers of oil at home by boring a hole in the ground, the grand old business of New Bedford is nearly played out.

A few American families still reside here, prominent among whom are J. H. Trumbull, M.D., brother of Rev. D. Trumbull, D.D.; the widow Crosby, from Ohio, and her son Wm. Crosby, who is the American Consul for this port; S. J. Stanton, and John F. Van Ingen, and others who are merchants. I presented a letter to Mr. Van Ingen from Rev. Dr. Swaney, and he entertained me most cordially as his guest during my sojourn. He is my right-hand man as collector and secretary of the school board we organized in Talcahuana. Dr. Trumbull is our most liberal patron, but Mr. Van Ingen is the more available for the hard work requisite for such an undertaking.

Rev. Dr. Swaney resided several years in this town, and gathered a fellowship band of about a dozen. They are scattered now, but so far as I could learn they cherish the mem-ory of their departed pastor, and are trusting in the Saviour. One of them, Mrs. Berry, died in the Lord a year ago. I met three of them, one of whom is a native, who wept as I talked to him about Jesus and his love. Another was an old American ship-master whom Bro. Swaney had, by the mercy of God, hauled up from the gutter when he was a poor stranded inebriate. My host told me about the reformation and steadfast life of the old captain.

One morning, walking along the beach, I saw a sober-looking old skipper, and said,

"Good-morning, sir."

"Good-morning."

"Have you lived long in this port?"

"Yes, sir, over twenty years."

"I suppose you knew Mr. Swaney?"

"Yes, indeed I did. He came to me when I was nearly dead. I was run down with drink, and given up by the doctor to die. But I had a dream some time before that I was drowning in the bay. The surf was very high. I made many desperate efforts to reach the shore, but was swept back by the receding sea. Finally, when I was sinking into hell, a great wave carried me to the land, and some one lent a hand, and I was saved; so I knew from that dream that I would not die at that time, and my hope helped me to live, when everybody thought I ought to die. Then Dr. Swaney came and told me about Jesus Christ, the Friend and Saviour of sinners. I was instructed by my parents when a child, but had apparently forgotten all these most important things. So I put my case wholly into the hands of Jesus, and he cured me, soul and body, and he has kept me ever since. Dr. Swaney left soon after. I was very sorry. I wonder that he has never written me."

"Have you no religious associates?"

"No, I have nobody to tell my feelings to but Jesus. I am talking to the captains and sailors here every day; I tell them about this great salvation, and give them some books to read, and pray for them. I do not see the fruit of it, but Jesus tells me to do it, and I know it will do good to some of them. The Bible is my constant study, and Jesus is my constant companion. Dr. Swaney gave me a Bible. I have read the Old Testament through four times in the four years since he left, and have read the New Testament through forty-six times. It is more and more interesting every time I read it, and God explains it to me in dreams. When I am on shore I go to church every Sunday, and worship God with the natives. I talk to many of them about Jesus, and they seem glad to learn these things. I am not a Roman Catholic, but there is no other worship here, since Mr. Swaney left, and I never debate with them, and God blesses me in talking to them and in worshiping with them."

I spent two pleasant hours with him, hearing his tales of varied experience and extraordinary dreams, and opening to his thirsty heart the fountains of Scripture truth. This is the kind of men whom the Holy Spirit teaches by "dreams"—persons not quite able to grasp the statement and spiritual meaning of God's truth, nor to discern the leadings of his Providence, and no man to explain them.

One night,- during my brief sojourn in Talcahuana, I preached twice in the fleet. The first service, was in the ship commanded by Captain Landsay, who is a Christian man, and regularly on the Sabbath conducts services with his men.   Our meeting was so interesting that the whole ship's company of officers and men accompanied me to the next service, which was on the vessel of another noble Christian gentleman, Captain Jeffreys.   At the close of each service I stated that I purposed to send a good man to Talcahuana to found a school, and hoped that he might also hold informal services for the seamen in this port, and that they might assist in raising a fund for his passage from New York, if they so desired. Without any begging beyond the simple statement of the case, they cheerfully subscribed fifty - two dollars at the two services.   Dr. Swaney's old captain was with us at those services, and professed to be greatly refreshed.

Mr. Van Ingen, who also was with us, was astonished at the lively interest manifested by the seamen in the services.

Said he: "I once went with a seamen's preacher to visit some ships, and the preacher, after talking a few minutes with the officers, said in the hearing of the common sailors, "If any of the men here are under serious concern about their souls, and wish to have a conversation with me, I shall be glad to talk to them.' Of course no one was disposed to confess there that he was in distress about his soul, and the visit of the preacher did not amount to much, so it seemed to me."

I find wherever there has been any earnest Christian work done on this coast, some life and verdure remain. Dr. Swaney is held in grateful remembrance here by hundreds of people. He is a superior preacher, and a sympathizing, winning man of God. I think, however, he has made three great mistakes in his ministerial life: 1st, when he left California in 1853, whither he had been sent by the Missionary Society of the M. E. Church; 2d, when he left Callao, about 1860; and 3d, when he left this coast again about four years ago. I don't know the standpoint from which he viewed these fields; that he acted conscientiously in leaving, and that he did good whither he went, I have not a doubt, but the killing need of the fields he left without supply is what strikes me. When a man of God is put into a most difficult unpromising field of labor, he should stick to it till he works out a grand self-sustaining success, or till he can see a better man for the work put in his place.

Talcahuana is the sea terminus of the "Talcahuana, Conception and Santiago Railroad," running a distance of 365 miles, through the great agricultural valleys of Chile, from Talcahuana to Santiago. The railway works are located at Concepcion, and most of the commercial business of this port is transacted in that city, which is ten miles inland.

The following partial exhibit will convey an idea of the commerce of this port: The number of sail vessels clearing the customs here in 1876, coasting vessels and foreign, was 182, with a tonnage of 38,428. Steamers, 163, containing an aggregate registry of 134,086 tons.

Value of exports for 1876—$8,613,164.

We cannot hope for a large number of English - speaking scholars in our contemplated school in Talcahuana, but hope to get many natives. One native gentleman gave us fifty dollars to help initiate it, and it is believed many of the higher-class natives will patronize it. It is a very needy field, which must grow into great importance, commanding, as it does, such superior transportation facilities both by sea and land.

P. S.—JUNE 11th.—Mr. Van Ingen has duly forwarded the passage funds, and I have appointed a thoroughly competent man, Prof. Haylett, B. A., to found the school in Talcahuana.

God bless the teacher, his pupils, and his patrons!

XVI.

This is a neat, compact town of about 20,000 inhabitants. I presented letters to William L——, Esq., a very influential resident of this city. He and his accomplished lady entertained me cordially. They emigrated from the city of London to this coast about thirty years ago. Their children, all except one daughter, have received their education in England. They could hardly consent to part so long with their last, and at once expressed a great desire for a good English school, requiring both a male and a female teacher. Previous abortive attempts, however, cast dark shadows over our path. Moreover many of their best citizens had not returned from their summer "watering-places," and all the merchants were absorbed in the wheat trade. Owing to a partial failure of the wheat crop in California, and a greater failure in North Chile, flour had risen to $13

234

per barrel, and hence a great rush in the wheat market.

The following Sabbath, the 24th of February, offered the only apparent opportunity of finding the business men at leisure, and even then they would most likely be off on tours of recreation. So I had my subscription-book ready, proposing to bring out two teachers—a man and his wife.

I depended on Mr. L—— to introduce me to the people. Noonday came, and he was not available. A grand specimen of an old-time London gentleman, overworked with excessive business as a merchant, and not hopeful of my success, he seemed reluctant to "come to the scratch." But soon after noon he returned to his house where I was waiting, and with him came Henry Bunster, Esq., to whom I had letters also. Bunster was my providential man for that moment, and had come sixty miles from his home, on other business, to be sure, but the Lord arranged to have him help me. I gave him my letters, and he at once recognized me. He was an old Californian, and had heard me preach on the plaza in San Francisco many times, and could never forget the scenes of those pioneer days in the history of San Francisco. I showed him my book, and he at once put down his name for $50. That struck a spark of hope in the heart of my kind host, and in ten minutes we were off to see what could be done. We called first on the "Intendente"— the Mayor—a noble native gentleman, and he unhesitatingly signed his name for $50.

Several leading native gentlemen subscribed each $50, and we should have easily raised $1,000, the amount we asked to bring out the teachers, and initiate the school work, but most of the men were absent.

Mine host could not command much more time for me, and through the ensuing week I could do but little, except to return to Talcahuana and raise nearly $400 and organize a school board there.

The next Sabbath, the only day we could get at the business men in Concepcion, John Slater, Esq., one of the American railway kings of the country, helped me, and by Monday morning our list exceeded $800. Many liberal men being absent, it was considered a sure thing. I appointed a small committee of three to proceed with the preparatory work.

This is a country of plentiful rains, verdant

hills, fine orchards, vineyards, and farms. I was glad to meet with an old friend in Concepcion, Captain W. S. Wilson, and make the acquaintance of his family. He is a nephew of Captain Wesley Wilson, who commanded the ship *Andalusia*, on which I and mine went to California in 1849. Captain W. S. Wilson ran the first sail vessel that ever went to Sacramento City; and on his second trip to that city took thither from the deck of the *Andalusia*, the "Baltimore California chapel," which my Baltimore friends had framed and sent with me. The captain is married to a Baltimore lady, who came with her parents to Chile when a child. They have a large family, and are liberal patrons of our school.

The one hundredth anniversary of the birth of "San Martin" was celebrated with great display of flags in the day, and illuminations at night, while I was in Concepcion.

What saint was he?

What little I have learned about him may be summed up in a few historical facts.

The war of independence for the South American Republics commenced in 1810. After four years of skirmishing, and some hard fighting, the Spaniards subdued and scattered the patriots. In 1817 San Martin, a native of Argentina, organized an army in his own country made up of both Argentine and Chileno soldiers. The great Andes ranges of eternal snow, like the Alps before the Carthaginian, stood between him and his oppressed brethren, but he brought his hardy men across the snow mountains, conquered the Spaniards and drove them out of the country. San Martin, and his brave officers and men, then marched up the coast, and rekindled the patriotism of Peru. After a struggle there of about four years, Peruvian independence, under the chieftainship of Simon Bolivar, was gained.

On the 29th of last December I visited the statue of that hero in the city of Lima. He is represented in a commanding attitude on horseback. I penned from the pedestal of the statue the following brief inscription, all in capital letters :

A·SIMON·BOLIVAR·

LIBERATOR·

LA NACION·PERUANA·

ANO·DE·MDCCCLVIII·

The date simply indicates the time when the monument was erected.

On the centennial birthday of General San Martin, Señor M. L. Amunátegui, Minister of Justice and of Public Instruction, made a public address extolling his services in the great achievement of emancipation in 1817. He said: "Our republic has not found traces of its origin among the tablets and parchments of ancient historic records, mounting to the gods as its progenitors, but finds restrictive laws that hindered industry, prohibited commerce, dulled intelligence, and declared it the colony of an absolute and despotic monarchy: the slave of a slave. . . . Besides the Spaniards, the Chilians had to contend with three formidable enemies, that counted more than legions numerous and well disciplined: these were prejudices, poverty, and ignorance. They could rely only on their own heart and arm."

Speaking of the battle of Chacabuco, in which San Martin defeated the Spanish army, February 12th, 1817, after crossing the Andes, Señor Amunátegui said: "For my part, the passage of the Cordillera was an achievement still more astonishing than those two days of battle crowned with glory. The leading of an army among the rocks and precipices, . . that.we call the Andes, is a deed of daring and energy that few generals have to show in their record of service."

The Spanish Government never acknowledged the independence of the Republic of Peru, though it did of Chile. In 1866, when the Spaniards were greatly in need of funds, they remembered the Chincha Islands as a paying concern, so they fitted out a fleet of seven war ships to proceed to the Pacific coast, and, under a show of law, which they termed "re-vindication," to take possession of the Chincha Islands. The results of that expedition against our cousins may be summed up in a few words:

1st. The fleet came to Valparaiso, and the officers were fêted, and grand entertainments were given to the admiral at the Chilean capital.

2d. The fleet weighed anchor and left, but the next news told the story that the Spaniards were in possession of the Chincha Islands.

3d. The Chilean newspapers took sides with Peru, and spoke out very freely.

4th. The fleet returned to Chile and demanded reparation for the insult. The

Chilenos maintained their ground, but tried to explain, and to vindicate their position. Their explanations were accepted by the Spanish minister of state, and it was supposed that they would hear no more about it, but in due time orders came from Spain, demanding the government authorities of Chile to salute the Spanish flag, and then treat. They refused to do anything of the sort.

5th. The Spaniards blockaded the Chilean ports, but a Chilean corvette captured one of the Spanish war vessels, which Cousin Chileno holds to-day.

6th. The Spanish fleet fired into the city of Valparaiso for three hours, burned the custom house and a few million dollars' worth of public property, and then sailed for Callao, Peru.

7th. The Peruvian batteries gave them a warm reception, and poured a hail-storm of cannon-balls into them, and it is said tore a hole twelve feet long in one of their ships. The fleet was thus kept so distant that not much damage was done to the town, and after nearly a day of mutual salutations of that sort, the Spanish fleet departed, and has not been seen in these waters since. There has been no reconciliation, and no friendly intercourse between these nations since, except that through the friendly mediation of our government they have agreed not to renew hostilities on either side without timely notice. The thing resulted in great damage to Spanish commercial interests on this coast. Our South American cousins are tremendous fellows to fight when their patriotic fire gets to a white heat. Their great weakness is in fighting each other.

In Concepcion we arranged to open a school, to commence with forty scholars, with good prospects of increase and permanence.

I had to leave on Monday morning, the 24th of March. I was sorry I could not remain longer to cultivate the acquaintance of the very intelligent and kind gentlemen, both foreign and native, whom I met in Concepcion, and who are the patrons of our contemplated school.

P. S.—JUNE, 1878.—I have secured for Concepcion three thoroughly good teachers— Prof. W. A. Wright, Miss Sarah E. Longley, and Miss Lelia H. Waterhouse, who are to sail from New York on the 1st of July proximo.

HOW OUR COUSINS ARE CONVERTED.

I said to a lady on this coast, "I knew

many of your people in the United States, and
I think they were all earnest Methodists."

"Yes, they were Methodists of the strict-
est sort, and my parents also.   They came to
Chile when I was a child.   My youngest sister
was not baptized till she was seven years old,
when Mr. Swaney came.   My mother never
would consent to let her be baptized by a
priest.   But when she grew up she became
engaged to a native gentleman, and could not
be married till she consented to be a Roman
Catholic, and in the process of converting her
they greased her with oil and salted her.

"So as my children are growing up in this
country, and will probably spend their lives in
it, rather than have them subjected to all that
nonsense after they are grown up, I have them
all baptized while little children by the Roman
Catholic priest.

"When they grow up, they can choose for
themselves."

The following notice of the baptism in Santiago of two English converts to the Roman
Church from Protestantism, says the *Record*, we
find in one of the daily papers, and translate it,
omitting the names of those concerned.   Of
these special instances we know nothing, only

in many similar cases marriage has been the converting ordinance :

"The neophytes, who know very few words of the Spanish language, sought the Rev. Father P. A. Valenzuela, friar of the order of Mercy, who is a complete polyglot, possessing about twenty languages, . . . a Chilian priest lately arrived from Ecuador. . . . The ceremony of baptism of adults is very curious. The postulants remained outside the church, and the priest from the threshold asked them what they desired.

"'The faith,' they replied.

"'The faith will give you life eternal,' answered the priest.

"Afterward he breathed three times in the faces of the neophytes, saying, 'Come out, unclean spirit, and give place to the Holy Spirit. Peace be with you.'

"Then he made the sign of the cross on their ears, mouth, eyes, nose and hands. Next he put salt in their mouths, as is done with infants, saying to them, 'Receive the salt of wisdom.' The catechumens knelt and repeated the Lord's Prayer. Father Valenzuela, taking them by the right hand, led them into the church, saying, 'Enter into the Church of God,

that ye may have right to life eternal.' The
Protestants cast themselves upon the ground
and repeated the Creed. This done, the priest
placed his thumb on the tongue and 'next
passed it over the noses and ears of the catechumens. Finally he anointed their breasts
with oil, he cast water on their heads, he put a
candle in their hands and a white cloth on
their heads, and after various prayers con-
cluded the ceremony."

In Peru foreigners wishing to get married
must have the legal ceremony performed by
the diplomatic minister, or a consul of their own
country, and then they can take their papers to
a clergyman, and get an ecclesiastical marriage.

In Chile, however, though in advance of
Peru in granting religious liberty, the foreigners are obliged to go to a Roman Catholic
priest for the legal marriage, and then go to
their own preacher. But in neither country
is a foreigner allowed to marry a native, except
by vowing to become a Roman Catholic, or by
obtaining a special dispensation from the Pope.
In the latter case bonds are given to bring up
the children resulting from the marriage in
the Roman Catholic faith. I heard of one
exceptional case in Callao. A Russian German

whom I visited in Callao, told me a part of his matrimonial experience.

Said he, "I became engaged to marry a Roman Catholic girl. I asked the priest if he would marry me.

"He said, ' I must consult the bishop first; come to-morrow.' So I called upon him at the time appointed, and he said, 'I have got the consent of the bishop, so if you will come to-morrow, I will marry you.'

"So I went next day to get married, but he said, 'I can't marry you to-day; come again to-morrow.'

"I went again, and he said, ' I am not ready yet; come to-morrow.'

"It was enough to make a good man swear, but I took it as patiently as I could.

"I went again at the time appointed, and the priest said, 'I can't marry you at all unless you sign an agreement to become a Roman Catholic.'

"I said, ' All right, I must get married at any cost.' He said, 'Very well, I'll have everything ready for you to-morrow.' I took with me some of my own people as witnesses of the marriage. The papers designed to bind me to Romanism were all ready for my signature, but he proceeded with the ceremony, and afterward said, 'Now sign these papers.'

"I said, 'I am a Protestant.'

"'But did not you promise to become a Roman Catholic?'

"'Yes, but with a mental reservation. I am nothing but a rough sailor, and don't make much pretension to religion; but you profess to be a minister of God, and yet you broke your promise to me four times, and I will break my promise to you only once.'

"'Ah, you villain! I am not going to let you off that way; you shall not have this woman for your wife.'

"I said to the girl, 'Are you not my wife?'

"'Yes, we have been pronounced husband and wife by the priest.'

"I said to my companions, 'Shipmates, are you not witnesses that I have been well and truly married to this woman?'

"'Yes, we are witnesses; we are ready to swear to that any day.'

"Then I said, 'Come, wife, let us go,' and away we went.

"I never troubled the woman about her religion, and she was a most amiable and kind wife to me for seventeen years, when she died."

XVII.

WE take the cars in Concepcion Monday morning, the 4th of March. The skies are bright, the air balmy and bracing. The wheat harvests have been gathered, and the dry stubble fields give the country a barren appearance, but this is relieved by the orchards and vineyards opening to view on every hand, loaded with fruit.

For forty miles our course is north-easterly, along the banks of the river Bia Bia, navigable for fifty miles by small steamers. Now we leave the river and strike northerly through the great valley of the Republic lying between the coast range of mountains and the Andes. It varies in width from fifteen to forty miles, with innumerable right-angular valleys extending far into the glens of the mountains. This is a great wheat-producing country. The fact is, with this climate and soil and the abundant

248

rainfall of every year in this latitude, they can grow everything that any market could desire. But from all we can see along this line of travel the cultivation is poor. Just look at those plows, two sticks of wood partly mortised and partly tied together with rawhide ropes. To this ancient contrivance a pair of oxen are attached, with the yoke tied fast to their horns. There are no handles by which to steady and guide the plow. Our farmer cousin simply holds on to the top of the upright beam, and guides the point of the lower end, which is supposed to do the execution in the soil. American plows have been introduced, and used in moderation in some parts, but they cost money, both to import, and to keep them in repair. This old Roman model, the same which is used in India, is a simple construction that Cousin Chileno can make, and repair himself, at no cost, scarcely, but a little time, and that is of but little value to him.

Moreover, Cousin Chileno says his plow suits the clay soil of this country better than ours. It can't turn the sod, but it cuts its little furrow trenches over six inches deep, through which the rains penetrate the soil readily.

11*

But our plowshare makes a smooth hard pan at the bottom of every furrow, which inter-feres both with the deep percolation of the water, and the penetration of the top roots of the grain.

And see those wagons, or rather carts. The wheels are simply six-inch cuts, sawn from a large log, and an axle hole bored in the center. The hole enlarges with use, sometimes more on one side than on the other, and such a creak-ing noise!—files and saws, or ungreased friction of hard substances of every sort—we can't get a figure of comparison to convey the idea; why, anywhere within a quarter of a mile it is enough to frighten the horses. I remember how the old carts of Valparaiso, twenty-nine years ago, made me stare and wonder. When I recently returned to Valparaiso and saw the fine carriages, street and rail cars, and not the track of one of these old wheelers left, I thought, Well, those old carts have had their day, and disappeared before the rolling advance of modern improvement; but here they are squeaking away, as in the olden time. Cousin Chileno says he can't afford to buy our big wagons, but he can go into the woods, cut down a big tree, saw off his wheels, and make a wagon to suit himself, and he likes it, so "every man to his liking, as said the old woman when she kissed the calf."

On and on we go for one hundred miles, and put up for the night in Chillan. The town, with its 22,000 people, is half a mile distant from the railway station, and here are a line of veritable four-wheel carriages waiting for passengers, so we take passage in one of them. They will charge a dollar most likely. We drive up to a French hotel.

"Driver, what's your charge?"

"Ten cents, señor."

Ah ! this is the old-time country, where the people earn their bread by the sweat of their brows, and have not yet seen enough of this fast age in which we live to learn how to charge exorbitant prices, and spend more than all they can make in "keeping up appearances." A stroll through the town brings us to the esplanade, where our cousins come out for an airing in the cool of the evening. It is a large and beautiful plaza with a fountain in the center, laid out with circular avenues, deeply shaded with a variety of ornamental and orange trees, and beautified by floral gardens. All the avenues are provided with plain, but comfortable seats with backs. Here they are, our strange kindred, some in fine attire, especially the ladies with their long trails. Many of the men and women are dressed in European costume, but a majority of them in the plainest native style. There a group of farmers from the country, and there a group of mountaineers from the Andes. We fall in with a few English railroad men, and among them our friend, Mr. Mero, the Canadian with whom we traveled from Panama to Callao. He recently removed from Concepcion to this place, being more convenient to his section of the railroad as an engineer. A few English people reside here, but not enough to sustain an English teacher or preacher.

No regular train to Talca to-morrow, but my time is too precious for delay, and the paymaster, my young friend C. H. Laurence, has given me permission to go with his assistant, Señor Cheveria, who goes through to Talca—one hundred miles—with engine and tender, to pay monthly dues to all the employés on that section of the road. He leaves at 5 A.M., so, to be ready for that hour of departure, I settled with my host—$1.50—for supper and bed before retiring for the night.

Being rather anxious, lest I should not come to time in the morning, I lighted my candle four times during the night. We get to the station ten minutes before time, and walk and wait for forty minutes. Mr. Mero came to see me off, and I presented him with a copy of "*Hymns, new and old.*" If truly saved, he would be a means of great good to our cousins. I hope yet to see him working for Jesus.

Tuesday morning, the 5th, we roll out about three miles to the river Nuble. The railway bridge across it, about a quarter of a mile in length, was swept away by the great floods from the Andes last June; indeed they swept away all the bridges on the line from this place to Santiago. The Nuble is not large enough for steamboat navigation, but at its flood, too large for the safety of any improvements within the breadth of its sweep. The new bridge is nearly finished. We walk across it, amid a crowd of workmen hastening its completion. Here we go again on a much larger tender, run before the engine, so that we escape the sparks and smoke. Our driver is a Mr. Allen from Paterson, New Jersey. He has his wife and four children residing at Linaris, a town of 6,000 people, on the line.

He was taking his tea as we came up, and kindly gave me "a horn," literally a pint of tea in a cow's horn. He kindly offered me bread, but having a supply, I simply accepted the horn of tea with thanks. Now the real interest of the day begins, the payment of dues to the railway employés. About every ten miles, where gangs of men are at work, the tender stops. The men come running, and stand ready. As each man's name is called, he responds and walks up, his money is counted audibly before him, and put into his hands.

Common laborers receive twelve dollars and sixty cents per month. A grade higher receive fifteen dollars. Foremen of gangs, nineteen; firemen, sixty; and drivers, one hundred and twenty.

On we go for another ten or twelve miles, whistle, and stop. Here the hardy fellows come and hear their names called, and receive "every man his penny."

On we go again. Its a grand holiday excursion. I have seen nothing lately so interesting. The scene can't be transferred to paper. There stands close by the paymaster a vulture-eyed-looking fellow watching his chance. His name is not called, but he grabs a lot of the money.

Just as it passes into the hands of the hardy
son of toil who earned it, that fellow lays his
hands upon it, and puts it into his own pocket.
There's one who has but two dollars of his fifteen left in his hands.   There's another who
stands with empty hands, and gazes at the
man who pocketed his pay.   His eyes say,
" It is too bad, but what can I do ? "

" Mr. Allen, who is that man who is gob-
bling the pay of these poor-fellows ? "

" He is the boarding-house master."

" Oh yes, I see.   He's the man who gets the
workmen round the ' board,' ostensibly to eat,
but really to drink up their wages before they
are earned."

Our seeming thing of life blows its great
whistle again, and we are off for another stage.
The interest keeps up all the way.   The most
popular man on the road is the paymaster.
They all seem so delighted to see him.   We
cross some of the rivers on a temporary side-
track, to be used till the bridges shall be rebuilt;
others which are larger we have to cross in
boats, and take another tender and engine waiting for us on the farther side.   We reach Talca
about three P.M., and put up at Hotel de Colon.

Talca is a pretty town, near to a river.   It

contains a population of 25,000. There are a number of American and English families residing here. I called on Mr. Holman, the miller, an American, and Mr. Bennett, the banker, an Englishman.

Rev. Mr. Curtis, of the American Presbyterian Board, is stationed here. He has in the cool season an English congregation of about forty persons. His native following, Mr. B—— says, "numbers six, and they are no credit to him." It is a hard field, but as needy as it is hard.

The plaza in front of our hotel is very beautiful. In the center is a broad, nicely-rounded plateau, covered with shrubbery and flowers, leaving space for an inner circular avenue furnished with seats, and a fountain sending up eight streams of water—four in the midst of a group of bronze statuary, and four more on the outer edge of the group, two from sea-shells, and two from pitchers, each held in the hand of the statue of a boy. About twenty yards north is another fountain and tank, another south, another east, equidistant from each other and from the central group, and on the west is an elevated stand for a band of music. Some of the tunes played in the evening soothed my weary spirit greatly; one tune especially, soft and plaintive, flowed upon me as I reclined in a conscious yet dreamy state, and it seemed to come away from beyond the clouds; I seemed to be quite on the verge of heaven.

Wednesday morning, the 6th, I took a third-class ticket 165 miles to Santiago. The high-caste ideas of the people of this country are such that a gentleman would forfeit his social standing in polite society if he should be seen traveling third-class. For the sake of my influence for good among such, I would, as far as practicable, shun the appearance of evil in their eyes; but here I was unknown, short of funds, and anxious to see the country and the country people, so the third-class was just the thing to my suiting. The cars were very long, a seat two feet broad, for a double sitting in the center, extending from one end of the car to the other, and a seat along each side. Instead of windows to obstruct the view and the fresh air, both sides were open, with a canvas covering to draw down in case of rain.

When not too crowded, I had a good promenade of about sixty feet. A few miles out from Talca we get out and descend the steep bluffs of the river Claro, and cross on a footbridge and ascend the steeps on the northern shore. Four arches of the wrecked bridge are still standing, but the remains of two or three central arches and their pillars lie in great blocks of ruined masonry down the stream. The bridge was at least ninety feet high. It will perhaps cost a million dollars to repair it. The work is in progress.

Here we are on another train, steaming away to the north. Such a crowd of our country cousins! It is surpassed only by a Pacific steamship load of the same sort. Every one seems to have all his personal property about him—bags, boxes, baskets and bundles of every shape; crowds of men, women and children, apparently emigrating, with all their effects, to climes remote. At every station, however, we part with many of them, and get their places filled up at once with new-comers. There comes a man with a basket of little chickens. He sits in a corner, and his chirpers keep up a perpetual complaint of hard times.

There comes the shoe and boot maker with a dozen pairs of his own make, with heels about two inches high. The people here seem to have a great ambition to rise in the world, and the bootmaker gives them an extra lift.

On we go from town to town. Yesterday we passed San Carlos, 5,000 population; Parral, 5,000; Lineris, 6,000; Talca, 25,000. To-day we pass Curilo, 6,000; San Fernando, 6,000; Raneaugna, 4,000; San Barmida, 5,000; and heave to in Santiago, which has a population of about 200,000.

My friend John Slater says, "With some one speaking the Spanish language to go with you, and introduce you to the people, you could found a self-supporting English school in every one of those towns." I should not be surprised if the Lord shall give me an order to do that thing one of these days.

A jolly set of people, these country cousins of ours, all in high glee, eating watermelons, apples, peaches, grapes, cakes and candies. We live well here at a very small cost.

Here they come again, crowding in, old men and maidens. "Give place to that dear woman with her child." She gets a good seat near the preacher. As we rush on her shawl parts, and the baby— No, it is a goose, with her long neck stretching out to see what it is all about.

There is a woman in the corner with great bundles of stuff, a little two-year-old girl, and a parrot. She appears to have a goose or a gobbler covered up under her shawl. Hours elapse, and not a quack from beneath the covering. Then, instead of another goose, a cunning-looking little cousin looks out on the scene with perfect composure. The dear little thing never cried a bit all the hot, weary way.

There comes a blooming "gushing girl from the country." She is dressed in a suit of nankeen, and wears a broad-brim straw hat. She gets her seat, and has a hearty cry to herself. Dear young cousin, she is thinking of the one she left behind her—perhaps her mother. Her tears, like the early dew, soon pass away, and now she is as jolly as her neighbors.

The great valley narrows; the snow peaks of the Andes stand out to view in solemn grandeur.

At sunset we fetch up in the dépôt of the capital of the country. I pay two and a half cents in solid cash, and get an upper seat on a two-story street-car, where I can see all that comes within the range of vision as we drive a couple of miles through the city. We alight on the grand plaza, and put up at the "Hotel Oddo."

At the dinner-table Mr. Parkman, the agent of the Philadelphia hardware merchant, with whom I traveled from Callao to Mollendo, sat down beside me. I was glad to see him again and hear that the merchants of Santiago had patronized him liberally, and had the night before given him a grand entertainment, largely attended by the merchants and other most respectable men of the city, many of whom, in their speeches on the occasion, expressed a great desire for enlarged fraternal and commercial intercourse with the "Great Republic."

After dinner I mounted the upper story of a street-car, and went for a call on Hon. Thomas A. Osborn, American Minister to Chile, who received me cordially. He was formerly Governor of the State of Kansas. He combines good abilities as a statesman with the modest, genial qualities of a gentleman and friend. He was well acquainted with Rev. D. P. Mitchell, of the South Kansas Conference, and other ministers who were particular friends of mine; so I spent a very pleasant hour with him.

Thursday, 7th, accompanied by Mr. Osborn, I went to-day to call on His Excellency Señor Annibal Pinto, the President of the Republic, and also on Señor Miguel Louis Amunátegui,

Minister of Justice and of Public Instruction.
Being in advance of the time for our reception,
we visited several departments of State, and
were entertained by their heads, who kindly
showed us objects of interest in the "great
house." We were then conducted to the department of the Minister of Justice and of
Public Instruction, and introduced to Señor
Amunátegui. He is about five feet ten, lean
and slender, with a broad, high forehead. His
appearance and address indicate a man of the
type of our Secretary Evarts. Señor Amun-
átegui·is believed to be the coming man for the
Presidency of the Republic at the next election.
I told him of my self-supporting economical
arrangements for founding schools in Concepcion, Talcahuana, and along the coast of
Chile, north, and in Peru. He said he was
very glad indeed to hear of my purpose, and
the success of preparation for its accomplish-
ment, and said he would be most happy to ren-
der every assistance we might require, or in his
power to give. A considerable conversation
ensued on the subject of education in North
America and in Chile.

He asked me if my wife was engaged in
educational work, adding, "If so, we should

like to have her take charge of a ladies' institution in this city."

I replied that my wife was fully occupied with her boys, and with her own household duties, but if I could be of any service to him in selecting and recommending for his school competent professors from the United States, it would be my pleasure to do so. He expressed thanks, and said he would consider the suggestion, and if he should find it practicable, he would communicate with me through Mr. Osborn.

We were next conducted to the department of the chief, and introduced to His Excellency Annibal Pinto. He is a man of medium size, not corpulent, but in good condition, with smooth round features, keen black eyes, with an appearance of great amiability and kindliness of heart, and a model of simplicity. He was seated at his desk, examining some documents as we entered, but arose and shook hands with us very cordially.

Mr. Osborn told him about me, and my mission to his country, and that I had a letter of commendation from President Hayes. His expressions of pleasure, congratulation, and assurance of support in regard to the English schools I was preparing to found on the coast were as emphatic as those of the Minister of Public Instruction.

He inquired particularly about Sr. Gmo. Laurence, of Concepcion, and other patrons of my work there. That is the city to which the president belongs, and his cousin, Major Pinto, is the treasurer of my school fund in Concepcion. After this conversation, His Excellency asked to see my letter from President Hayes, and read it over with close attention, evidently not on my account, but because it was from the hand of the "President of the Great Republic." We did not ask nor desire any government funds for our school work, but thought it well to secure for it the friendship and moral support of those distinguished men; they both belong to the "Liberal party," and meant all that they said about our schools, in which religious creeds would "not be interfered with, nor taught."

Both of the two great political parties of the country are nominally Roman Catholics, but the Liberals are working for a divorce of Church and State and release from the controlling power of the priesthood, especially in the departments of education, and of the government, and to cur-tail their monopoly of so much of the real estate and moneyed resources of the country. The Liberals are growing into power more and more, and as they drift from Rome it is a matter of the greatest moment to them and the peoples of their country that the clear light of a pure Gospel shall shine upon them, and enable them to keep off the fatal reefs and rocks of infidelity and atheism. Voltaire's works have recently been printed in the Spanish language, and are, I am told, extensively read by the people of Chile. Satan's missionaries are not trammeled by any conventional rules, nor tied down by the red tape of perfunctory authority, but proceed in their diabolical work on every breeze and by every current of commerce to the ends of the earth. The organization of the Church of Christ, and of its benevolent societies, and its administration of law and discipline, and its various orders of ministers are all of Divine appointment, to facilitate, but in no way to retard, the spread of the glorious Gospel of Jesus "to the uttermost parts of the earth." In utilizing indigenous resources for the advancement of the kingdom of Jesus Christ, we may learn useful lessons from "the children of this world, who are in their generation wiser than the children of light."

A letter of commendation from the President
of the United States was of value to me as a
stranger in a strange country. It came to me
in an emergency when I needed a friend, just
the time I always get special help from God,
often from an unanticipated source. I never
thought of applying to the President of the
United States for a letter. I applied to our
Church authorities on behalf of South America,
and tendered my services without any cost to
the Church; but they seemed to think that the
time had not come, and I had to proceed wholly
on my own responsibility, as I had done in
India, not breaking any law of the Church, but
proceeding so far beyond organized lines or
established precedent as to be considered "out
of order." Having no authority from Church
or State to proceed on a mission to South
America, this unofficial letter of friendship
came to me in this wise:

My old friend, Chauncey Shaffer, Esq. (of
New York), was pleading a case before the
United States Supreme Court, in Washington,
and meeting with President Hayes, told him
of my contemplated visit to South America
to open fields for educational and evangelical
work. The President replied that he had been

"well acquainted with Mr. Taylor's work for many years past," and gave Bro. Shaffer the letter commending me and my work in South America.

On Friday, the 8th of April, in company with Mr. Parkman, I came first-class across the mountains and down the valleys, over one hundred miles, to Valparaiso, where an un-doubted welcome awaited me at the home of my dear friends, Dr. and Mrs. Trumbull.

XIX.

TRAVELING in the rail-cars in India, on one occasion, I spoke to a gentleman seated beside me, and soon discovered that he was a Roman Catholic. I said to him, "As I am an older man than you are, and have seen much of the world, there may be portions of my experience that would be interesting, and perhaps profitable to you. If it is your pleasure to hear me talk, I will not require a reply nor ask you any questions."

"Very good, sir; I will listen with pleasure."

"When a boy, I learned to earn my living on my father's farm, and had fair educational advantages and good religious training. As I grew to maturity I became greatly impressed by facts like these: the Maker and Preserver of this world is a great king. I know not the extent of His kingdom, but this world is a part

268

of it, and He daily manifests the great interest He feels in it—He cares for oxen, feeds the sparrows, and the fish of the sea, from the minnow to the leviathan, get their food from His bountiful storehouse: 'He openeth His hand and satisfieth the desire of every living thing, as a farmer gives food to his fowls.' If He takes such interest in His live stock, what must be His love for His subjects and children!

"In analyzing my own conscious being, I observed, 1st. That I had an animal nature with its appetites adapted to my material relations to this world.

"2d. A soul nature with its instincts and appetences adapted to the body, and its purposes and relationships to the present life.

"3d. A higher spirit nature with a capacity, powers, and aspirations adapted to my civil relations to God as my king, and filial relations to God as my Father. As He has provided so munificently for the wants of our bodies, surely He would not fail to provide for the wants of our higher spirit nature. First, as a foundation of all right loyalty to my king, and fair-dealing with my fellow-subjects, He would certainly give us plain laws defining the relations we sustain to God, and to each other, and the duties growing out of them.   I had some skeptical thoughts discrediting the authority of the Bible as God's book for man's instruction in these things; but it seemed to me as incredible that God would give us eyes and give no light adapted to their purpose, as that He would give us a conscience, and furnish no authoritative reliable standard of right for its guidance.   However emphatically the heavens may declare the glory of God, and the book of nature all around us show forth His marvelous works, they do not give us the moral laws essential to the instruction of the human conscience.   The demand is imperative, and nothing in the book of nature is taught more manifestly than God's adequate provision, and marvelous adaptation of supply to demand—light for the eye, air for the lungs, the modulations of sound for the ear, water for thirst, food for hunger, and so on. In correspondence with all this there must be a supply equally adequate and available for our higher spirit nature.   That nature is invisible, God is invisible, His spiritual supplies must be invisible, but we require a visible book of instructions—a book containing a revelation of God to man, and a revelation of man to man, intelligibly manifesting the information concerning God and man essential to good citizenship as His subjects, and to the realization of His higher purposes in regard to us.

"I found that the Bible was the only book that could set up any tenable claim to be of Divine authority. It has its vulnerable points, but that is what we might expect from the fact that human agency has been employed in its primal revelation and record, and its transmission from first to last. Hence while its essential truth is retained in all its entirety and harmony, its drapery, in passing through the ages, has been somewhat soiled and marred, but for practical purposes it is clearly intelligible, and immutably reliable, as God's authoritative book for man's instruction.

"I got the idea early in life that it is not the medical book that cures the patient, but the medicine; not the documentary credentials, but the doctor—in short, that the Bible, in its relation to God and man, and the whole breadth of its teachings, bears a similar relation to the subjects of which it treats, to that of any other book. A book on astronomy, for example, does not contain beneath its lids the planetary system. I hence perceived that possibly the essential truth of the Bible was demonstrable consciously in human experience as really as books on mechanics and navigation. All such books are studied, not for speculative, but for practical purposes. There may be a hundred diagnostic delineations of a hundred diseases in the medical book that a sick man cannot understand. His only concern is to find his own case described, and to verify the truth of the book by a successful application of the prescribed remedy. So the mariner studies, and applies his books on navigation; so the mechanic verifies daily the truth contained in his books along the line of demonstration.

"Thus in the practical study of the Bible I became more and more impressed with the fact that God is a sovereign, and that I am a responsible subject of His realm; and as such, bound to study His laws. His synoptical exhibit of the moral law—the ten commandments impressed me much. Addressing the human race individually, He says to me,

"'I am the Lord, thy God.' My sovereign, my Father, the only object worthy of my supreme confidence, loyalty, and love, and the only supply for the demands of the capacity and powers with which He has endowed me, and which are essential to my eternal relations to Himself. Hence, His *second* command, 'Thou shalt have no other gods before me.' Could He consent to such seditious dishonor to His government, and such debasement and ruin to me as a subject? Hence, in the *third* commandment He guards the gates against rebellion by a warning not to take His name in vain, or injure His reputation in the minds of others, or lessen the weight of its influence in my own.

"As he had given me the mental appetence for property, had given me the right to accumulate it, and the right to have and to hold it, with a profusion of property resources worthy of Himself, He kindly, in the *fourth* commandment, adjusts the division of time between the demands for toil and the recuperative rest essential to the life and continued working effectiveness of the toiler. He gave us six days out of seven for all the purposes of secular work, and in mercy to man and all beasts of burden, retained in His own right one-seventh of time, and set it sacredly apart as a day of rest. The Sabbath is doubly freighted with blessing to man; to secure more certainly the needed rest of his active mental powers from the care of secular associations, and to have his spirit specially refreshed by undisturbed communion with his Creator, He has appointed the rest day of each week as a holy day—a levee day of the king, when He is delighted to see us with clean hands and clean clothes, with our wives, children and friends, come into His courts, and, in blessed intercourse with Him and each other, receive His smile and special benediction.

"To encourage our obedience to his Sabbatic law, He assures us that He Himself, after the work of six days, 'rested the seventh;' so that we should not think it a matter of small import, but a physical necessity for man and beast, and spiritually the highway to honor and bliss traveled by the king.

"The *fifth* commandment is to protect the honor of father and mother, addressed to every child—'Honor thy father and mother,' with the promise of length of days, and a land of plenty, to make long life a blessing to us.

"The *sixth* commandment is to protect life —'Thou shalt not kill.'

"The *seventh* is to protect an institution of pristine Eden, under the divine sanctions of which the human race was to be propagated, and every resource belonging to it conserved for its legitimate purpose—'Thou shalt not commit adultery.'

"The *eighth* is to protect our property rights. Having given us property rights and resources, and six working days per week in which to accumulate property, how Godlike and kind to take an inventory of our effects, and set upon them the broad seal of His protective law, backed by penal sanctions which ought to make the bones of every thief and defrauder rattle in their sockets!

"The *ninth* commandment is to protect our reputation, the most valuable possession pertaining to this life that we can acquire—'Thou shalt not bear false witness against thy neighbor.'

"The five commands of the second table of the law just named notes each the highest offense against those varied God-given rights of man.

"The *tenth* commandment strikes at the lowest. It is designed, on the principle that 'an ounce of prevention is better than a pound of cure,' to nip the first bud of lust in the soul that would lead to a violation of any of them.

"These laws are equitable, reasonable, right, essential. They pertain to eternal relationships between God and man, and between man and man, and hence, of perpetual obligation

through all time and through all eternity.
They breathe naught but love and good-will
to man, and all men should honor God and
keep His commandments.   I always admitted
the obligation, but unhappily when about five
years old I commenced breaking the commandments of God, and went on for fifteen years in
wicked rebellion.   I often tried to do better,
but encountered two difficulties: First, as a
rebel, I had forfeited all the rights of citizenship, and had become obnoxious to penalty.
The law was all right, but I was all wrong.
Everything depends on which side of the law
we are on, the protective side of loyal obedience, or the penal side of disobedience.   I
found that the law can do nothing for the law-
breaker but execute its penalties upon him in
the interest of society.   It was of no use to
hope in God's mercy, for He is not simply a
Father, but a king, and I was a rebel, and He
is bound to execute penalty, maintain law,
and protect society.   So all my attempts at
obedience were like a felon under sentence to
be hung, trying to repair his felonious breach
upon society till the day of his execution, and
then the sheriff takes him out and hangs him.
Another difficulty in my case was that my

nature was so corrupt, I could not reform myself.   My attempts were as futile as those of
an Ethiopian to wash himself white.   So I
was in a sad state.   I saw clearly that there
was no power in any human resource to meet
my case.   Then on the great divine principle
of demand and supply, I searched the Bible
more carefully to see if God had revealed a
provision by which He, as a righteous judge,
could acquit a guilty man, and whether he had
a provision by which a nature so perverted
and so polluted could be purged and purified,
and brought back to filial union with Himself.
Seeking light with a sincere purpose to walk
in it, the mysteriously wonderful, but glorious provision of salvation for sinners, through
the incarnation and blood-shedding of Jesus
Christ, opened up to my mind as the only
provision that could by any possibility meet the
case.   As a basis of faith I read the prophetic
record of God concerning His Son.   I found
that hundreds of years before He was manifested
in the flesh, the holy men of old who had been
saved by Him, and inspired by His Holy Spirit,
had foretold His incarnation, and described
His humiliation most minutely, so that there
should be no mistake in identifying the long-

expected Saviour of sinners. They wrote out
plainly where He should appear in the world
as a babe, and develop manhood among men,
that he might on the plane of human experi-
ences and within the radius of human percep-
tions manifest God to the world—the mind of
God, the feelings, the love, the sympathy of
God to men; also the principles of God's immutable truth and justice as applied to men in
His providential government, and God's methods
of dealing with all classes of men, and especially His method of saving sinners from their
sins, which was the great object of His mission
into the world. So I found those old prophets
had foretold all the great events of His life,
and of His death, and of His resurrection from
the dead; and of His mediatorial mission in
heaven and His soul-saving mission on earth, to
be maintained till the day of final judgment. I
then read carefully the historic record of God
concerning His Son, and found an exact correspondence between the prophecies and the
facts as they transpired in the Person and sur-
roundings of Jesus of Nazareth. It was a
satisfaction to find that the documentary credentials of this great Redeemer of mankind
were so clear and credible, but to me in my

carnal darkness, they seemed like the credentials of an old medical doctor long since deceased.   The papers are all right, but where is
the man to answer to them?   Thus I groped
in the dark for a long time, but finally I became associated with intelligent godly men
and women whose testimony would stand in
any court in the nation, who solemnly testified
that they knew Jesus Christ; that though
'He was dead, He is alive again for ever-
more;' that He is a real Person, and as accessible now as when manifest in the flesh, though
invisible like the air we breathe, yet none the
less real, and as truly the Saviour of sinners
now as He was eighteen hundred years ago:
that all we read of His saving acts are recorded teaching facts, which are an index to
His immutable character, and to the methods
of His saving work among men to the end of
the world.   Thus, by the word of God which
I had read, and by the testimony for Jesus
which I heard from these witnesses, I obtained a reliable basis of faith in the Lord Jesus
as the Saviour of sinners; and on these evi-
dences, I consented to take His easy yoke, and
received Him as my Saviour, and trusted Him
to do for me all that was in His heart to

do for me. It was on the 28th of August, 1841, that I fully surrendered myself to God, and accepted Christ.

" The great Redeemer took my case in hand at once, and through His merits and mediation I was acquitted from the penalties of the laws I had broken, pardoned for all my sins, notified of the great transaction by God's Spirit in my heart, and had my vile nature changed—the lusts of the flesh purged out, and the fruits of the Spirit put in. I was so filled with love to God, and sympathy for man, that I began the next day to tell all whom I met about the Saviour whom I had found. From that time to the present I have been traversing continents, crossing oceans, and witnessing to a personal verification of the truth of the Bible record concerning Jesus Christ, to a personal demonstration of the fact that He is alive, and the Saviour of sinners, and that He saved me from sin, and, in spite of all temptations and trials, preserves me from sinning. Thus I have been all these years, cultivating a personal acquaintance with Jesus, so that I know Him better than I know any man in the world, and have seen many thousands of sinners in all the zones of this globe, test and verify these truths and facts, in like manner. He is no respecter of persons, hence what He has done for me He is anxious to do for everybody, and for you, my dear brother."

At that point the train stopped at the station at which I had to leave it. As I rose to start, my Roman Catholic friend grasped my hand with tears in his eyes, and said: "It is a most fortunate circumstance that I came on this train and fell in with a man like you. I never heard such good news before. I am sure I shall never forget your words, and I am greatly obliged by your kindness in telling me these things." My heart was full of love and sympathy for him. I learned afterward that he received Jesus and spoke of this conversation, and testified to a personal experience of salvation in Jesus.

XX.

POOR OLD SAN SEBASTIAN.

THE recent tribulations of the patron saint of Yumbel in South Chile, and of his friends, are graphically set forth in the Chilean daily papers, as follows:

The Record says: "A letter appears in the *'Revista del Sur'* of Concepcion, which may interest some of our readers who are unfamiliar with the extent to which the religious simplicity of the Chilean people is carried, and the way in which their credulity is exercised. The letter refers to the robbery of the image of San Sebastian from the church of Yumbel.

"You are aware that St. Sebastian is the patron saint of this town, and by his numerous miracles, which amount to not less than fifteen or twenty thousand a year, has achieved a fame rivaling that of Our Lady of Andacollo.

"Every year, on the 20th of January, a grand mass is sung, a sermon preached, and processions formed in his honor.

"On the 19th, 20th, and 21st of January the people repay the saint for his miracles—payments which have reached the enormous sum of $11,000, but have this year only amounted to $5,600, doubtless owing to the general scarcity.

"The usual manner of making offerings to the image of St. Sebastian, is for the giver to advance on his knees for a distance of two or three cuadras, the blood streaming forth and the pilgrim fainting at every step.

"Somebody formed the idea of stealing him, and yesterday a door of the church was found open. On the sacristan being informed, he went and made a search, and found that the image of the glorious Sebastian had disappeared.

"As it was Sunday, there were people in the church, who before mass was celebrated heard these terrible words from the priest:

"'With the profoundest sorrow I have to announce that last night the most horrible sacrilege was committed. Our patron saint San Sebastian has been stolen, and I beg my beloved flock to denounce to justice or to me the names of the guilty parties.'

"The people, on hearing this, cried out, burst

into tears, and exclaimed against the heretics, who they said were doubtless the robbers.

"About 10 A.M. all the inhabitants of the city were in the streets, weeping and lamenting. At last an attempt was made to discover the hiding-place of the saint, with which object about three hundred persons went to the river and the neighboring fields.

"About three in the afternoon a man arrived at full speed with the information that the diadem or crown of the saint had been found. The man was quite smothered with questions, and a new army was speedily on the march to the place indicated, where they found a fire had been kindled. There the pedestal was found, and a bottle which, from the smell, had evidently contained paraffine.

"At nightfall the people, excepting a few who remained to watch suspected places, returned to the city with great rejoicings for the discovery of the pedestal, which they kissed, shedding abundant tears, and cursing the heretics.

"That night nothing else was spoken of but the saint, and the savages who had stolen him.

"About eight o'clock next morning it was

cried aloud in the streets that the saint had appeared, half burnt, and buried in a sand-drift, at a distance of some twenty cuadras from the town. Then there was nobody, with the exception of the heretics, who refrained from going to the blessed place. Men and women fought for the privilege of kissing the charred lump of wood. Thus they arrived at the church."

Another witness, writing to the *Revista del Sur*, says :

"You are aware that Sebastian is the patron saint of Yumbel, and for his numerous miracles, numbering not less than fifteen or twenty thousand, rivals Our Lady of Andacollo. Every year, on the 20th of January, mass is sung, a sermon preached, and booths erected. On the 19th, 20th, and 21st 'the people pay the saint for the miracle;' payments have amounted to the large sum of $11,000. This year, however, they have only reached $5,600; the falling off is due to the prevailing scarcity. People come approaching the saint on their knees a distance of three or four hundred yards, leaving tracks of blood, and frequently fainting.

"Some one took a notion to steal him; yesterday a door of the church was found open, and the sexton, making search, missed the image of the glorious Sebastian. It was Sunday; some people came to the church and heard from the curate these terrible words: *A most horrible sacrilege has been perpetrated! Our patron St. Sebastian has been stolen, and I beseech my beloved flock to inform the courts, for me, as to who may have been the offenders!*

" Hearing this the people shouted, burst into tears, and declaimed against the heretics, who, they said, had doubtless done it. By 10 A.M. the inhabitants of the town were all in the street crying and shouting. An effort was made to find the saint, and three hundred persons went in search. About three o'clock a person came at full run, bringing word that the crown had been found. He was overwhelmed with questions. A new crowd went to the place where the crown had been discovered and found that fire had been burning. The pedestal of the image was discovered, and an empty bottle that had contained turpentine. Night came on, and almost everybody returned to town with great joy at having found the pedestal, which they kissed, shedding tears and cursing the heretics. That night nothing was talked of but the loss of the saint and the savages who had stolen him; more than one, it is said, called on the judge to indicate to him the persons they suspected. About eight o'clock this morning it was announced with loud cries through the streets that the saint had been found half burned and buried in a sand-bank half a mile from the town! Every one then, except the heretics, went out to the sacred spot. Men and women contended for a chance to kiss the burnt block of wood. Thus they reached the church."

The curate of Yumbel speaks as follows of this affair in his note to the Bishop of Concepcion, dated February 3d: "With profound sorrow I inform your Grace that last night there has been perpetrated the most scandalous and sacrilegious robbery in the parish church. Thieves entering the church through the vestry climbed to the altar of our Father St. Sebastian, and bore away the saint with his pedestal, weighing not less than sixty pounds. . . . The tracks on the altar cloth were evidently made by a foot wearing a fashionable boot, and this, coupled with the fact that nothing was taken except the saint, leads me to believe this scandalous thing has been done by people of good standing. . . . The state of my mind does not permit me to enter into further details; but to-morrow I will give your Grace further facts. I simply inform you of the calamity which has imbittered my heart on the very day of my coming into the curacy.

"BALDOMERO PRADENAS, Curate."

Two days afterward the bishop sent the following in reply, dated February 4th, Concepcion: "Your note, giving account of the impious and sacrilegious robbery of the statue of St. Sebastian, has been received.

"The act is horrible, and the idea that it could be perpetrated in a Christian community, leaves intense sorrow in the soul. Impiety, however, ruling in the miscreants that have perpetrated this crime, knows no limits in its excessive perversity. Not only as the bishop of the diocese, but also as a citizen of Chile, I deplore this savage and odious sacrilege which shames and disgraces my country. Oh that justice may display all its zeal and activity in discovering and punishing the evildoers! I, for my part, will do what is possible in my sphere of action, and to that end send a judge, appointed to institute the appropriate investigation touching the fact and the incidents connected with it. Do you, for your part, convoke the people, that they may offer, in the Lord's temple, humble petitions in extenuation of the offense which has been done to His Supreme Majesty. Repeat with the people for three days the Litanies of all the Saints, with the Prayers of the Ritual, *For Whatever Tribulation;* expose for an hour the most Sacred Host, and ask and seek, with the faithful, mercy and pardon for this most grave scandal. Have confidence, and God will return for the honor of His cause humbling the wicked. May God keep you.

"JOSEPH HIPPOLYTUS,

"Bishop of Concepcion."

In a note to the bishop of February 5th, the curate gives the following further details: . . . "The theft of the statue of the glorious martyr St. Sebastian took place on the night of the 2d in the church itself. As was to be expected, the people of Yumbel were profoundly alarmed, and on the 3d inst., Sunday, commenced search for the beloved image. Fortunately some ornaments of silver were left on the road. These ornaments, illustrious sir,

13

served to guide the people in their search. Divine Providence aimed once more thus to defeat the hateful and cowardly plans of impiety.   In fact the people, in their distressful anxiety, followed the road toward the southwest, and after finding in the public square a silver bracelet which the saint wore on one of his arms, and in the suburbs his crown, discovered also, half a mile from the town, the pedestal of the image, the girdle, and a bottle that contained a residuum of paraffine. Two of these things had been scorched with fire. . . . The day following the statue was found with one arm broken, and the rest of the body charred. It was brought back by the people to the church, where I received it with the religious ceremonies that seemed befitting. The occurrence has filled my heart with sadness, and a religious people with consternation and alarm. . . . It is a sacrilegious profanation of our churches, a brutal attack on our worship, a mockery of our beliefs; the work of shameless impiety peculiar to that Satanic hate which the enemies of the Catholic Church have to the religion we profess. The authors of this crime cannot be common thieves, but must be men of more elevated position, immoral, impious miscreants, and this explains all. . . . The image of the saint was found with a rope round the neck, which seems to show that these new iconoclasts dragged it, even, on the ground, in the sacrilegious frenzy of their rage."

XXI.

THERE are many thousands of these industrious, thrifty people in South America.

In Chile according to census returns there are nearly 3,000; but that estimate does not include their children. As a rule, a German has a wife, as every competent man ought; and the Germans generally have large families, so that the children born in Chile of German parents would largely outnumber the old stock from "de faderland." There are two principal German colonies in Chile, the larger is in the Province of Valdevia. The city of Valdevia is its largest center of population and commerce. I was very anxious to visit those German settlements in that province, and made partial arrangements to have Brother Müller accompany me, but found that it would require more time than I could possibly command. Brother Müller visits them frequently, and is just the man to introduce Christian

ministers among those of them who have none.
The following is substantially his statement,
the result of his frequent visits among them :

In Valdevia there are over 2,000 Germans,
only about one-eighth of whom are Roman Catholics. The other seven-eighths are nominally
Lutherans. They are a well-to-do people and
have good schools, but no minister, and have
no special desire for one. They are positively
opposed to religion, according to their conception of it.

In the neighborhood of Valdevia there are
about 1,000 more Germans; three-fourths of
whom are Lutherans, but not much inclined to
be religious. There are only about a dozen
English-speaking people in Valdevia.

Las Ulmos, five hours ride from Valdevia,
contains about a dozen German families.
Three of those families only are Roman Catholics, and they seem more hungry for the Gospel than their Protestant neighbors.

There is, however, a German school there,
in which the Bible and Catechism are used.
There is no pastor to look after these few
sheep in the desert.

La Union, about a day from Valdevia, on
horseback or cart, contains about 700 Germans;

there are about 300 more within an hour from the town. These are a very amiable people, and ready to receive the truth, but have no minister to impart it.

Osorno contains a large German population, about 2,000 in the town, and 500 more in the neighborhood. They have an ultra Lutheran minister. There are two principal merchants there who speak English, and who are the leading supporters of the church. Three-fourths of these people are Protestants. A day's journey from Osorno brings us to *Lake Llanquihue.* It takes about five hours by steamer to cross the lake. Around this lake there are 160 German families. Two-thirds of them are Protestants; they all seem hungry for the Gospel, and greatly desire to have a minister. "I have meetings in their houses," says Müller, "and they keep me singing and explaining the Word of God, and praying with them, till one o'clock at night. They are a very kind people. It would cost a minister nothing, beyond a moderate rate of traveling expenses, to live among them. His regular board anywhere in this region would only be $10 per month, but here in the country he would pay nothing."

There are eight families living south of the lake who have a little church and an old minister, Rev. Mr. Godfrey, who is also a farmer. *Puerto Montt*, on the coast, south of Valdevia, contains about 1,800 Germans. They have a Lutheran minister, Rev. Mr. Schenk, who also teaches a school. *Ancoot*, a port about four hours of steamboat travel north of Puerto Montt, contains about a dozen German families. The port for Valdevia, *Corral*, contains also about a dozen German families. The large majority of these people are farmers, and well-to-do traders, and able to support Gospel ministers and churches, if godly men could be sent to them who could command their confidence and do them good.

The other German colony embraces two towns, *Angol* and *Los Angule's*, containing about 500 Germans each, besides many more in the surrounding country. Mr. Müller has not visited these, and they have no minister or spiritual guide of any sort. Besides these colonies there are many Germans in every large town in the republic, and the same is true of all the republics of South America, especially in Brazil, with fifty German colonies, which contain a German population of

40,000. Most of the English people of South America will live and die in it, and their children after them, but they don't mean to. They came to make money and return to England or Scotland to enjoy it. The mass of them fail to save enough to enable them to realize their dream of home life; and many of those who make a fortune and return to England, find everything so changed, and they are themselves so changed, that they soon become dissatisfied and return to their more congenial clime in South America. But the Germans come to South America, just as they go to North America, to stay and make a permanent home for themselves and for their children, and are becoming, and must more and more become, a potent homogeneous element of South American society. Their industry, economy and intelligence, with good schools everywhere for their children, will make them an influential and powerful people in all these republics. If supplied with thoroughly godly, evangelical ministers now in their forming state, now while more accessible than they are ever likely to be in later years, a large proportion of them can be won for Jesus. They will thus constitute a grand medium of access to masses of the

natives, and a powerful self-supporting working agency to enlighten and save them. If
we can find young German ministers in
America, suited to this great pioneer work,
the whole cost would not exceed $500 each,
to pay passage and initiate them in their work.
I would agree to put in a dozen of the right
men at that cost. It is an insult to these
people to offer by charity to supply any of
their wants. They are able to provide for
themselves so far as funds are concerned, but
they have not the knowledge of the men they
need, nor the desire for them sufficiently strong
to lead them to seek shepherds. They are
wandering sheep far out in the desert, and
need true self-denying shepherds, led by the
great good Shepherd Himself, to go out and
seek them. If they should go with plenty of
missionary money and educate the people into
the habit of receiving it, and of having very
much done for them that they ought to do for
themselves, some good would result, no doubt,
but a much higher class of agency can be enlisted, and a much greater work accomplished
on the self-supporting principle from the start,
except a small amount for the transportation
of the ministers to these needy fields.

13*

XXII.

On my way south, Rev. Dr. Trumbull called my attention to the great need of a seamen's preacher for this port. His church and others had always been open for all classes, yet but few sailors attended. Twice for a short time, many years ago, they had a preacher for seamen who did a good work, but did not remain to carry it on. Rev. Mr. Lloyd, a couple of years ago, fitted up a hulk as a Bethel for seamen, and held two services in it, when a gale sent the hulk to the bottom of the sea, and seven persons living aboard of it were drowned.

Mr. Müller, the Bible agent, when able to command time from his extensive agency through the country, visits the shipping, talks to the seamen, and sells them books.

Two laymen also go occasionally and hold little services in the forecastle of some of the ships, but we greatly need a man who knows

298

how to adapt himself to sailors to come and devote his time to them. "Now," continued the Doctor, "if you will open a subscription for funds to bring out a good man to labor among the seamen of this port I will head the list."

I am sure, from what he said, that he meant to give us a hundred dollars.

I thanked him for his liberal proposal, but replied, "Doctor, the seamen are neither paupers nor heathens. If they want a preacher, they are able to pay all the expenses involved, both in his transit and support.

"The way to interest seamen really in such an enterprise, and have a thing that will live, is to have it originate with them, and be run by them. All we want on the land is a resident, trustworthy committee, consisting simply of a president, secretary, and a safe deposit for their funds, as an anchorage for sea-faring workers while in port." By this time I was rather committed to a test of the principle of utilizing the indigenous resources available in the fleet of Valparaiso.

On Friday P.M., March 15, Mr. James Blake, an earnest Wesleyan, but a member and worker in Dr. Trumbull's church, got a boat and put me aboard the ship *Santiago*, Captain Mills, but, under a press of business, he immediately returned to the shore, so I was in the fleet, but knew nobody in it.

On inquiry I learned that the master of the vessel was absent. The first mate, however, said that I was welcome to hold a service if I desired to do so.

He called the men aft, and I preached to them in the cabin, but the captain not being aboard, I did not present my subscription-book. It was now getting dark, and they having but recently arrived in port, could give me no information in regard to other ships. I wanted to make a sure strike at the start, as much depends on a good beginning. It is said "a bad beginning makes a good end." That is true in some cases, but a good beginning, well conducted, is better. The mate of the *Santiago* had the boat lowered subject to my order.

I said, "Men, pull me to the ship *Eden Home*."

"Ay, ay, sir," and the hardy fellows very soon sent me up the ladder of the *Eden Home*. I introduced myself to the captain, and he introduced me to his wife. The captain consented that I should preach after tea to his men on the deck,—a quiet, kind gentleman, Captain J. H. Randolph. On their invitation I took tea with them. Meanwhile Captain W. T. Ditchburn, of the bark *Egremont Castle*, and his wife, came aboard on a visit, and were delighted to hear of the contemplated service, and suggested that it should be held in the cabin, where "we can have good seats and good lights." The master at once cheerfully consented. Tea over, the men were invited, and filled the cabin. We had some hearty singing, and I preached to the small, but very attentive company. Afterward I told them what I proposed to do, and presented my subscription-book. Times hard, freights very low, and no better prospect ahead, but the captain headed the list with five dollars and the crew added fifteen—twenty dollars.

Captain Ditchburn invited me to preach aboard his ship the following evening, which I did, and he and his men subscribed twenty-six dollars.

On week-days the sailors are at work, so that we cannot, ordinarily, have a service for them till after they get their supper, so my hope of success was in the services of the ensuing Sabbath, March 17th.

Captain Ditchburn met me with his boat at the pier Sabbath morning. The wind blew heavily, and rendered it very difficult to get about in the shipping. The gale however, blew from the land, otherwise the sea would have been too rough for small boats. It was a dark morning for my enterprise, and I was strongly tempted to give it up.

We boarded the bark *Mary Moore*, Captain W. A. Nelson. He had only a few men aboard but received me very kindly, and I spoke to him and his men in the name of the Lord. At the close, I could but tell them what I had thought of trying to do, and they responded cheerfully, and subscribed nineteen dollars.

Captain Nelson then ordered his boat to take me to the ship *Coronilla*, Captain Wm. Davis. He had but a small crew; but we had a good service, and they subscribed nineteen dollars. By invitation of Captain Davis I dined with him, and then he sent me to the bark *Santiago*, Captain Wm. Moffat, and, after preaching, he and his crew subscribed thirty-five dollars.

I preached next on board the ship *Valparaiso*, Captain Alexander Mills, and they subscribed twenty-four dollars.

I had an appointment to preach for Dr. Trumbull at half-past seven that evening, and my dear friends, Captains Moffat and Mills, accompanied me to the shore. The spray swept over the boat's company, and had not Captain Mills wrapped me up in a large oil-cloth cloak, I should have been in a bad pickle for an appearance in the Union Church. - It was so rough my friends simply put me safely on land, and at once returned to their ships. We had a fine audience in the evening, and a gracious illumination of the Holy Spirit.

On Monday evening I conducted a service on board the *B. Balmore*, Captain John Davis, and twenty dollars were subscribed.

On Tuesday P.M., we held a meeting of the captains, whose interest we had enlisted in the work, in the upper room of Williamson, Balfour & Co.'s store. Dr. Trumbull presided. After due deliberation they all agreed that my plan was perfectly plain and practicable, and unanimously adopted the articles of agreement I had submitted constituting THE VALPARAISO SEAMEN'S EVANGELICAL SOCIETY. They elected Rev. Dr. Trumbull President, and Mr. James Bloke Secretary, and voted that the funds should be deposited with the house of

Williamson, Balfour & Co." Captain Ditchburn and Captain Mills were appointed collec-
tors while they should remain in port, which
office they cheerfully consented to fill.

The meeting voted an appropriation of funds
for the passage of the minister whom I shall
select and send, and that till further order, he
shall be paid one hundred dollars per month
for his support. They wished to give more,
but I preferred to have all my men commence
as low in the scale as one hundred dollars per
month. There are over twelve hundred arrivals of ships in that port annually. If only
ten per month will pay twelve dollars each,
they would sustain this simple economical plan
of work. We don't propose to buy any hulks,
nor build anything on the land. Every ship
under this kind of ministry becomes a *Bethel:*
every ship's company a congregation within
hailing distance, which, at any hour between
meals on Sabbath, or on any evening in the week,
can, in one minute and a half, be assembled for
an informal religious service. I bade adieu to
my loving, earnest co-workers—the captains and
men who are pioneers in this work of God for
the seamen of those waters—and on Wednesday
the 20th of March, 1878, I set my face home-

ward to find the men whom God has selected for my various fields in South America—a dozen men and about half a dozen ladies.

P. S.—I may add that the Lord had them in readiness on my arrival, and the man for Valparaiso turns out to be a young man combining rare scholarship with all other qualities suited for that work—a classical and theological graduate of the Boston University—Rev. Ira H. La Fetra, B.A., B.D. The idea has obtained rather extensively that an old condemned hulk in a harbor, or some old barn in an obscure alley of a port city is the place in which the men of the sea, the bravest men in the world, "ought to worship." I have in mind now an old shell of a frame and board house, better suited for a stable, bearing on the unplaned surface of one of its boards, in large letters, this appeal to the affectionate consideration of the men of the sea—" *Sailors, this house is for you.*"

Many seem to think also, that the best preacher for seamen is some old blunderbuss no longer fit for use on the land ; especially if in his early life he had been before the mast a voyage or two. I would not at all underrate the good accomplished in the past or that may be

done in the future by any variety of means or
agency; nor would I for a moment discourage the
use of hulks or barns as places of worship, alike
for seamen or landsmen, nor the employment
of any suitable agency, however humble; but
I do emphatically enter my protest against
any invidious distinction between ladies and
gentlemen of the land, and gentlemen of the
sea and their families. On the water, the
home of the sailor aboard a modern clipper
ship is equal, in the style and finish of its
architecture, to anything on the land; no better place afloat for a seamen's Bethel.

When the Lord Jesus dwelt visibly among
men He exhibited a special interest in seamen.
He explored the globe to find a dozen men on
whom He could confer the exclusive responsibility and honor of apostleship in His kingdom,
and one-third of His selection were fishermen-
sailors; and they became the most distinguished of His apostles. Every sailor ought
to take to this old friend of the seamen, sign
His "articles," and be loyal to Him to the
death. His grand work of bringing all nations
into His kingdom challenges, and should enlist
the heroic adventurous spirit of every sailor.
The men of the sea truly converted to God,

and purified from sin, would constitute a grand body of missionary agency which, led by the Holy Spirit, would soon carry the Gospel testimony "to all nations."

In our great work among seamen in Calcutta, every ship's company saved by the Lord Jesus are at once organized into a church on their own ship, just as St. Paul organized churches in the dwellings of the people—the church in the house of Stephanus, in the house of Gaius, in the house of Aquila and Priscilla, of the Elect Lady, and others. We have about fifty such organizations on that number of ships that voyage to and from Calcutta. On every departure their preacher writes to ministers residing in the port to which such ships are bound, and bespeaks their attention and interest in the floating church on its arrival.

Thus a year ago, when I was laboring in San Francisco, I received a letter from Rev. Dr. Thoburn, in Calcutta, saying that the ship *Knight Commander*, from Calcutta, with twenty-two converted seamen aboard, would be due in San Francisco in June, etc. Such organized bands of godly seamen escape the landsharks, and receive a welcome by Christian ladies and gentlemen in every port, and mix freely in their assemblies in blessed fraternity. It is not money as a charity that the sailor needs nor desires. He earns his money by the sweat of his brow, and can pay his own way, and is willing to do it, and do as much to help the needy according to his means as any class of landsmen; but the sailor needs the same kind of sympathy and wise winning attentions of intelligent Christian agency which is necessary to win any other class of persons to Jesus; and the general treatment, according to character, to which landsmen, by the rules of good society are entitled.

XXIII.

I BADE adieu to dear friends in Valparaiso on Wednesday morning, the 20th of March, and embarked on the steamship *Itata*. One day's steaming brought me to Coquimbo, where I opened a field for a minister, as before stated. On the night of the 24th I embarked on the P. S. N. Co.'s steamer *Lontue*, 1,848 tons register. She has five powerful steam "winches," two on each side, fore and aft, and the anchor winch, all worked from the steam boiler of the ship. The four freight-lifting winches can all be worked at once. They sling twelve bags of flour every time, containing 2,400 pounds, and anything above that weight up to ten tons, so that loading and discharging is executed with great dispatch.

Now let us take a view of the ship. The hold is full of heavy freight—flour, sugar, salt, and all sorts of merchandise and timber. The

309

main deck is packed with live stock. Near the forecastle on the " starboard " side is a flock of sheep. From the space occupied by the sheep back to the stern of the ship there are 130 mules, wedged in as closely as they can stand. On the "larboard " side are 30 or 40 mules and about 100 bullocks. On the upper deck, aft, is the dining saloon; and forward of the smokestack, on each side, are the cabins of the first-class passengers, and all the rest of the deck is occupied by the coast traders—consisting of half a dozen provision merchants, male and female, with a large following of clerks and servants. Their stores consist of cheese, butter and bacon, watermelons, squashes and pumpkins, turnips, potatoes and onions, and such onions as never were seen anywhere else, except possibly in California; apples, pears, and grapes; some also have boots, shoes, and dry goods. At every port their customers come aboard to buy, and for hours the deck is one great bazar, and many boats are loaded with those Chilean products. The traders are generally very quiet, glad to see their old customers, and conduct themselves very creditably, and are a very useful class of people. They pay large freight bills to the steamship companies, and supply tens of thousands of people in the dry ports of Bolivia and Peru with the necessaries and the luxuries of life. The company has recently passed an order, for the safety of their ships, to clear the upper deck, and confine the traders to the main deck. The steamship *Tacna* a few months ago left Valparaiso with about a hundred passengers and a full freight, and when but a few miles out, there being a heavy swell, her top load so far exceeded her ballast that she rolled over and sank. She had on her upper deck, thirty-three thousand water-melons and a freight of pumpkins, and all else in proportion. Only three persons of the whole ship's company were rescued.

This order to clear the upper deck was to take effect on the first day of April. On that day the traders on our upper deck having nearly sold out their stock were removed, and crowded along the outside and rear of the dining-room. It looked like a prompt execution of the order, but the fact is the removal of the traders was to make room for beef cattle and bulls for baiting in Callao. Two hundred and fifty bullocks and bulls were hauled in by the horns at a single port, and when there was not space on the main deck into which to shove another one edgewise, a hundred of them were slung up and landed on the upper deck to take their place with the first-class passengers, and I must say to their credit that they behaved themselves well.

We have been looking at the main and upper decks, but still higher we ascend to the hurricane deck. Here we have the highest seats in the synagogue, for such as are inclined to sit on the deck, or on a box or bundle. This deck, save "the bridge" of the officer on watch, is from stem to stern crowded with the deck passengers.

At one port one hundred and thirty came aboard in one gang. They were "miners on a rush for new diggings," a thousand miles up the coast from where they embarked. Ninety tickets had been issued for eighty men and ten of their wives, but it was found that one hundred and thirty were in the crowd. The first mate, a tall determined New Yorker, is ferreting out "the stowaways." They are all round him, and all talking at once, and swinging their arms about him, but he never flinches for a moment, and now he marches thirty aft in spite of all their remonstrances and sends them ashore.

A difficult task, executed with great tact. Not a blow was struck, from either side. If one had been struck no one could have counted the number that would have followed, for they were all at the white heat of unreasoning passionate excitement. Next day ten more stowaways were detected and sent ashore.

The remaining crowd were rather sulky, till the New Yorker set them to remove a few cords of cabbage from one part of the "upper deck" to another. He thus won their confidence, and with something to do, the spell was broken, and from this time they were the jolliest lot on the ship.

I spent a few days of successful toil in Callao and on the 13th of April took passage for Panama, with our old American friend Capt. Hall, the Commodore of the P. S. N. Co.'s fleet. In Panama I was well entertained at the Grand Hotel at a cost of three dollars per day. Spent one day in Aspinwall and got a subscription of $56, payable monthly, for the support of a minister to labor in that needy town. I left the subscription in the hands of Mr. Peter Austin, who wrote me by the following mail that the subscription had grown to $86 per month, and that he expected further success, so that I shall D. V. send a minister of the Gospel next September to labor there.

Mr. Mosely, the P. M. S. S. Company's agent, and manager of the Panama Railroad, kindly gave me a passage first-class thence to New York at half fare. I did not ask nor expect such a favor, but was thankful, though for five nights I encroached on the reserve space of the steerage passengers, and slept on a pile of sails near the fore peak where I got the full force of the breeze. My whole fare home, first-class, cost a little less than my outward passage in the steerage. Arrived in New York on the third day of May, six months and sixteen days from the date of my departure for South America, and found a joyous welcome awaiting me at the home of my dear brother Chauncey and sister Shaffer. During my brief absence, by the miraculous mercy of God, I traveled about 11,000 miles, and opened the twelve centers of educational and evangelizing work described in these pages, to which I am appointing eighteen earnest workers, twelve men and six ladies. On my visit to the Boston University, a few days before my departure,

I requested Alexander P. Stowell, one of the graduating students, to act as my recruiting sergeant for the enlistment of first - class workers for South America. During the first week after my arrival, Prof. Stowell sent me the names of eight candidates who were ready for orders. I felt a desire that, in addition to all other qualifications for their work, they should be singers and teachers of vocal music. It turns out that they all, in that, as in everything else, are just the men whom God has selected for this most delicate and difficult work. The ladies too, are well educated, experienced teachers in all desired branches of education, including instrumental music.

I said to one of our elect ladies, "Are you willing to go to Panama, and teach school for the Jamaica people?"

"Yes, Bro. T——, I will go anywhere."

They are a people despised by some white folks, who derisively call them "Jamaica niggers."

"Will you share their reproach, and teach their children?"

"Certainly I will, if you decide to send me there."

I added, "But, my dear sister, it has the

reputation of being a very sickly place. In the construction of the Panama Railroad 'tis said that three thousand workmen died in making the first seven miles of the road.

"In attempting to drive piles to secure a foundation for the road they dropped in a shipload before they found occasion to use the hammer of the pile-driver. Each pile as it was let go slipped through out of sight; they could scarcely see the place where it went through, so I don't know how many missionaries may have to be dropped in there in preparing the way of the Lord. Can you risk your life in such a place?"

"Yes, Bro. T—— I am not afraid; I will go to Aspinwall, or Panama, or to any place to which you may assign me."

I arranged to have her accompany Prof. Wright to a most healthy climate in Chile.

Miss L. H. W., the young lady who accompanies her, is also a highly educated accomplished lady, and daughter of one of our ministers. I wrote her explaining that in our poverty of financial resource, my workers would have to go as steerage passengers as far at least as Callao, a distance of three thousand five hundred miles, and in answer received the following letter from her, which I take the liberty of inserting as an illustrative specimen of the spirit of the workers God has given me for His South American mission:

———"I am very glad that Jesus is so kind, for I am very strengthless. He will never break the bruised reed. He surrounds my life with His love as with a mantle. He fills my heart with His abiding presence. I have consciously given myself to Him, and am consciously accepted of Him. In all my experience He has never allowed anything to come upon me more than I could bear, but sometimes all that I can bear. He knows how to adjust everything so nicely. I go forward to my seed-sowing work without a shadow of fear in my heart. Doth not perfect love cast out fear? Does this seem like boasting? I do not mean it so.

"God is very great, I am very small. In spite of my frailty it is easy for Him to save and keep me. I dare not go one step alone, but with Him at my side and my hand clasped in His why need I fear? It is blessed to trust.

"My box leaves to-day for New York, directed as you requested. I shall certainly hope to see you when I arrive there. I do not think that

God chides me because my heart aches so, and the tears come at thoughts of leaving every friend. It only shows that I love them well, and yet I love Him more. Why should I fear hardships? My Jesus had not where to lay His head. I have always fared better than that. He became poor, and I through His poverty became rich; He wandered foot-sore and weary, with no resting-place, and through those wanderings millions have found rest. Do you suppose that He is sorry now as He sits by His Father and sees throng after throng of white-robed ones kneel before Him? Is He sorry that He knew what it was to be poor and hungry and tired and misunderstood and mocked and crucified? He groaned beneath a weight of sin that I might go sinless and free. He had no home in order that I might have a shining mansion. It seems to me that if I had ten thousand lives they would be none too many to consecrate to His service. I do not say this to boast. It comes from a full heart. 'My highest place is lying low at my Redeemer's feet.'"

THE END.